INKY:
Seeing Eye Dog

(Original title: Inki)

by Elizabeth P. Heppner

Illustrated by Tom O'Sullivan

SCHOLASTIC BOOK SERVICES

NEW YORK • LONDON • RICHMOND HILL, ONTARIO

For Richard

Copyright © 1957 by The Macmillan Company. This edition is published by Scholastic Book Services, a division of Scholastic Magazines, Inc., by arrangement with The Macmillan Company.

1st printing .... September 1967

Printed in the U.S.A.

Contents

An Unwelcome Visitor   5

A Frightened Puppy   13

An Unusual Offer   21

Work and Play   33

A Round-Robin Letter   48

A Visit to the Kennels   58

"Intelligent Disobedience"   72

"Merry Christmas!"   90

Home at Last   100

Unhappy Days   109

An Important Decision   116

A Wonderful Surprise   126

Note to the Reader:
   A New Home for The Seeing Eye   136

An Unwelcome Visitor

JONATHAN JONES jumped out of bed and snapped
on the light.

There was trouble somewhere on the farm.

He listened intently. That was it: a frightened
cackling from the chicken coop that sounded like
a string of firecrackers going off in the early dawn.

Jonathan fought back the urge to return to his
warm bed and steal a few more minutes of sleep.
But it was that irksome sense of responsibility that
made him get to his feet, pull on his clothes and
the fur-lined Air Corps jacket his father had sent
him from Korea. After all, he *was* head of the house
while his father was away.

5

He opened the door quietly and paused in front of his mother's bedroom. She was asleep. He decided not to get the shotgun which hung on the wall by the bedroom fireplace. Instead, he slipped quietly downstairs, unbolted the front door of the farmhouse, and went out into the chilly dawn.

He followed the sound of the frantic cacklings, past the large red barn to the cluster of buildings beyond. By the pigsty, Jonathan heard Old Growler oink quietly in her sleep. Nothing had disturbed her! The goats were restless but asleep; there was no sound from the cows and horses in the barn. Only the chickens needed him.

Jonathan remembered the fox barks he'd heard lately. With the weather turning cold and food for the wild things becoming scarce in New Jersey hills, fat hens would make a tasty breakfast for some fox.

He thought, "If only I had a dog at my side."

He was a little frightened now, as the noise continued, and he knew he heard something larger than a fox moving about in the coop.

Jonathan reached the henhouse just in time to see a stooping figure creep out of the shadows. A tall young man emerged into a patch of moonlight.

He had a hard, crooked mouth, and he carried a gun. Jonathan found himself looking right into the barrel.

"Stay where you are, kid. If you tell anyone you saw me, I'll come back and shoot you."

Then the young man turned and loped off toward the pasture and the fringe of woods by the stream. Jonathan was too frightened to move. He stood frozen to the spot, watching the man crash heavily through the willow thickets and on into the woods.

Suddenly Jonathan was aware of annoyed cluckings from the coop. His hens were peering at him from the open door. Jonathan quickly went into their house and secured the door. Old Smathers, the rooster, confident once again in the presence of his master, gave a rousing crow of victory. The hens clucked around the rooster; it was Smathers, not Jonathan, who had saved them from the invader.

Jonathan made a quick count of beaks and found the thief had stolen two of his best hens. The boy was very angry and fought back tears. He was very fond of his chickens, because he had raised the seventeen biddies and the rooster from eggs as part of his 4-H project at school. The money he earned from the eggs still meant, someday, a German shepherd dog. Now the money meant a winter

8

coat, schoolbooks, perhaps a few dollars toward Christmas.

As he sat on the floor with them, the brood began to calm down and to move around him. He spoke to them softly, clucking, throwing feed to them. Finally his favorite biddy, Miss Victoria, came and perched on his knee. She scolded softly. Jonathan scratched her neck.

"Miss Vic, someday — someday we're going to have a dog around here to help me protect you. He would have warned us about this."

Miss Victoria preened and pecked her master gently. She was hungry and coaxing for food. Eventually Jonathan rose, fed and watered his chickens, fastened the latch, and returned to the farmhouse. The light was on in his mother's room when he trudged upstairs.

"Jonathan, what's wrong?" her voice was anxious.

He ran into her room. "Oh, Mom, a thief stole two hens. He had a gun. He told me not to tell anyone I'd seen him, or he'd come back and shoot me!"

Mrs. Jones got out of bed and reached for her dressing robe. "Are you all right, Johnny? He didn't touch you, did he?"

The boy reassured her that the thief had only

killed his hens. "But maybe, Mom, if we'd had a dog, he could have protected us."

Mrs. Jones pushed her curly black hair back from her eyes and shook her head.

"Jonathan, your father left us a perfectly good rifle for that purpose."

Her son was impatient. "But a dog, Mom. I want one so badly. Just to have. And he could help me run the farm and protect you."

His mother laughed. "Oh, Johnny, I know. I know how much you want a dog. But with Dad away, you and I have to be careful about money. If you had a dog, you'd have to feed him good food. If he were sick, you'd have to take him to a veterinarian. We just don't have the money, Johnny."

Jonathan knew the argument by heart, but for the first time he sensed a weakening in his mother's determination. She was worried, too, about that man with the gun.

"The dog could have half my food, Mom," Jonathan persisted. "And we do have extra eggs and milk."

Mrs. Jones kissed her son lightly on the top of his head. "Jonathan, I want you to grow up to be a fine, healthy boy. You can't share your meals with a dog. Please, let's be patient a little while longer, till Dad comes home."

"When, Mom? How long do they keep prisoners of war?"

"It can't be too much longer, Johnny. Two years is such a long time."

The boy nodded. They both missed his father very much.

He must ask Officer Fairbarn again when he thought the war in Korea would be over. Officer Fairbarn, the village policeman, had been in the other war and knew about such things. Jonathan also thought he'd better tell him about the chicken thief. His mother agreed.

"Mom, do you really think that fellow would come back and shoot me?"

"Just let him try," Mrs. Jones replied. "Remember how I winged that chicken hawk with Dad's gun? First shot, too."

Jonathan remembered. His mother *was* a crack shot. They'd had so much fun together, before Dad left. Yes, he'd be very glad when his father came home again.

His mother stood up and gently pulled him to his feet. "Come on, Johnny, we've got a workday ahead of us."

Together they went about the early-morning farm chores. After breakfast, Jonathan watered and fed the animals and milked the cows. Mrs. Jones had started her household work when her son picked up his lunch and schoolbooks and kissed her good-bye. Then he started the long walk to school, down the dirt road and into the village. The last bell was ringing as he reached Valley View School. He had a good excuse for being late. Officer Fairbarn had been more than interested in Jonathan's chicken thief!

A Frightened Puppy

When Jonathan returned from school that day, there was a New Jersey State police car parked in front of the farmhouse. A trooper with a rifle was talking to Mrs. Jones, and another, in the driver's seat, had his short-wave radio tuned in to headquarters. Jonathan could hear it sputtering as he jumped the picket fence and ran toward his mother.

"Jonathan, these men want to talk to you about that prowler you saw this morning," she said.

Jonathan could not keep the excitement out of his voice. "Yes — yes sir?"

"Just relax, Jonathan, it's all right," the policeman said quietly. "Officer Fairbarn reported to us immediately, and we found your chicken thief camped down by the stream on the far side of your property."

There was a long pause. The officer looked questioningly at Jonathan's mother.

"It's all right," she said, "I never keep anything from my son. You may tell him the whole story."

The officer continued. "Well, Johnny, you were lucky. That fellow is a pretty mean character. He has been in a good deal of trouble, and we have been looking for him for a long time."

The trooper patted his rifle. "We cornered him down by the stream, and he will be put away where he can do no more harm. But now we want to ask you a question. Did that fellow have a dog with him?"

Jonathan frowned. "No sir, he was alone, absolutely. I would have known if he'd had a dog."

Mrs. Jones laughed. His mother's laugh was infectious, and Johnny grinned. "Of all the fourteen-year-old boys I know, Officer, Jonathan would certainly have known if there was a dog in the neighborhood. Any day now I expect to wake up and find one in bed with him."

The policeman laughed and thanked them both. The driver contacted headquarters on the car radio.

"Burns and Mead reporting. Tell Mac — sorry — no sign of Inky. That is all. Over."

Then they touched their caps and drove away.

That afternoon, while Jonathan went about his chores, he dreamed of the battle he had missed right down on his very stream bank. He wondered, too, what sort of a dog the prisoner had with him.

That night the wind blew up, and the first real frost of autumn seemed to be moving along on the air. Jonathan curled up by the fire, but he soon found it difficult to concentrate on his homework. He'd been at school during all the excitement, and now he'd have to wait till Monday to tell Charlie and the gang all about it.

His mother's voice interrupted his thoughts.

"Jonathan, bedtime. I'm going to turn in now. Saturday's a busy day."

Jonathan stirred from the warm hearth chair, stretched, then reached for his jacket. He knew he had to go out to the stream and see it all for himself. He called up to his mother.

"I'll just check around outside, Mom, and then I'll be right up. Good night."

Before he heard any protest, Jonathan was outside and running fast toward the stream. The boy followed the path he knew so well, guided by a

15

full moon above. The stream ran almost black along the smooth, slimy stones, and Jonathan was aware of the sounds of deer and other animals starting on their evening quests for food and water.

As he climbed the stones toward the barricade, he imagined the sounds and voices. Jonathan ducked behind a tree and imitated the policeman's deep voice:

"Hey you, up there. I'm the law. Give yourself

up. You haven't got a chance."

"Whannng! Smell that gun powder."

"Got him, first shot!"

"Drop that gun, you crook. Here we come, over the top."

Jonathan paused, ready to charge the barricade, when he heard a faint, sharp whimper.

It was an animal noise, but it didn't sound like the wild cries of woodland creatures. It wasn't quite like a fox bark or the throaty hoot of an owl. The whimper started up again, and Jonathan knew it was a dog. Yet somehow it didn't sound like an

ugly, snarling cur, the kind the criminal might have owned. This dog was in trouble. Jonathan plunged through the willow thicket toward the sound, which had stopped again. Then the boy remembered the name, Inky, the police mentioned over the radio. He stood still and whistled. Then he called:

"Here, Inky, Inky."

He was rewarded by a series of yelps, then by a higher wail that spoke of hunger and cold and loneliness.

Jonathan followed the yelps as they grew louder. He reached a clearing well back from the stream and saw by moonlight the remains of a campfire. It was probably a second campsite the thief had built, undetected by the police. As he approached, Jonathan saw a black mass huddled near a log. Jonathan walked cautiously toward it. Holding out his hand, he felt a coat of soft puppy fur. A cold nose nuzzled his palm, and then a warm tongue washed his cheek.

"Hello, Inky," Jonathan murmured, holding the little animal close to him. He saw that the puppy had twisted itself in the rope that tied it to a bramble bush. The choke knot was cutting cruelly at its throat.

Now the puppy began to tremble. The boy felt

ribs sticking out along the shaggy sides. He untied the rope, picked up his little bundle and tucked it into his jacket. The puppy was heavy in spite of its poor condition, and the walk home was slow.

There were no lights in his mother's room when Jonathan reached the farmhouse, so he went directly to the kitchen. He poured milk into a saucepan and put it over the coal stove, still warm from banked embers. As he waited for the milk to heat, he inspected his puppy.

She was a female German shepherd, about three months old, and just the kind of a dog Jonathan had wanted all his life. Her fur was matted but soft. It was jet black, except for surprise patches of brown under her tail and belly. Her feet were splotched with black and tan, and a bar of tan crossed her chest as if it marked a place for a halter. Inky's eyes were brown, and very bright and merry. She had a smiling mouth.

When Jonathan gave her the milk, she drank it noisily, wagging her tail as she lapped. She polished the plate with great care and then made a quick, happy lunge at Jonathan's shoes. Suddenly, in the midst of play, she whimpered. Jonathan saw then that she favored her right paw. He leaned down and found a slightly festered place where a thorn had become imbedded in the pad. Carefully he took Inky's paw, held it firmly, and withdrew the nasty-looking thorn. Inky did not move. Her mouth quivered, but she watched him with trust. Then she started to lick her wound, and Jonathan knew that now she could take care of it.

He lifted Inky quietly in his arms and they went upstairs together to his little dormer bedroom. Here he showed Inky pictures of his mother and father. He showed her his 4-H diploma and ribbon he had won raising chickens. Then he quickly put on his pajamas, washed in the little basin near his dresser, and dove into his warm featherbed. Inky was up and under the blankets with him in a flash.

He said his usual prayers, and thanked God for sending him Inky.

"And please, dear God, let me keep her," he added.

All night Inky slept soundly at Jonathan's feet.

An Unusual Offer

JONATHAN AWOKE. His mother was calling from the kitchen. "Time to get up and feed the biddies, Jonathan. Breakfast's ready."

A sudden squirm at the bottom of his bed brought Jonathan bolt upright. It wasn't a dream after all. Inky was here in bed with him. His very own dog. He ducked under the covers, made his way down to her, and put his arms around her.

"Hi, Inky. Good morning!"

She wiggled from head to tail, and her warm tongue brushed against his cheek. Suddenly he heard his mother's muffled voice directly above him.

"Jonathan, what have you got in bed with you?"

Mrs. Jones prodded her son gently, then felt

along toward Inky. The covers flew off the bed and the two of them, boy and pup, sat up to face her.

"It's Inky, Mom."

"Oh, Jonathan, what a darling pup. But where did it come from?"

Jonathan recounted the night's adventure. Then he looked toward her for a final word of approval. She sat down, one arm around her son, the other around Inky.

"Jonathan, I just don't know how we can afford her."

The boy interrupted: "Mother, let me earn extra money. I can baby-sit, over at Charlie's. Maybe we can have a roadside vegetable stand next summer. And maybe — you know Officer Fairbarn said he doesn't think the war in Korea can last much longer. There's talk of a cease-fire."

Mrs. Jones smiled. "Did he say that now? It sounds hopeful."

"Then what about Inky, Mom? Shall we try?"

Mrs. Jones looked at the puppy athwart Jonathan's knees. She looked up at her son's intent freckled face and mop of red curls. Then she gave up.

"All right, Johnny, we'll try. But first, I want you

22

to take Inky to Officer Fairbarn. She looks like a good pup, and perhaps the thief stole her. We want to know if we can keep her, legally, before we make plans."

Jonathan hugged his puppy. Half of his prayers seemed to be answered. But he knew his mother was right about the law.

That morning he dragged his chores out as long as possible before paying a call upon Officer Fairbarn. He cleaned Old Growler's sty with meticulous care, and he even scrubbed her back for her. Old Growler had to meet Inky. So did the cows, the chickens, the horses and ducks. Inky kept close to Jonathan and just smiled. Jonathan noticed she met animals halfway. If they drew back, she ignored them. If they were friendly, like Miss Victoria, Inky was very pleasant in return. Even the Outside Cat who lived in the barn finally accepted Inky. The Outside Cat, a large tortoise tom with white vest and ringed tail, at first arched his back and hissed. Later, following the two about the barn and studying Inky from the safety of the rafters, the Outside Cat finally came up to the puppy, rubbed noses, and burst into a tremendous purr of welcome.

Eventually Jonathan knew it was time to take

23

Inky to the village. He found an old leather belt of his father's, which he looped around her neck. Bidding a glum good-bye to his mother, he started out in search of Officer Fairbarn.

As they walked along the quiet country road, Inky led the boy gently, but she didn't tug at the lead. She carried her head up, with ears cupped, nose occasionally sniffing among the fallen autumn leaves. Jonathan was proud, as proud as he'd ever been in his life. He whistled happily, and Inky pricked up her ears and looked back at him. She wagged her tail, as if keeping time.

Jonathan heard the sound of an approaching automobile and edged over to the footpath. The car, coming from behind, passed him and then came to a sudden halt. It was a police car. The boy and his dog stopped while an officer jumped out and came toward them.

"Where did you get that puppy, young man?"

Jonathan caught Inky up in his arms. "I found her, sir, on my property. Last night."

The policeman said sternly, "Better get into my car. I think you have a stolen dog there."

Jonathan's worst fears were confirmed. Then Inky *did* belong to someone. He hugged her to him as they squirmed up on the front seat of the patrol car. The policeman turned around, raced past Jonathan's home, toward the hills. Grimly he flicked on his radio:

"Flannagan reporting. I think I've got that stolen pup. Found it with a boy near Valley View. Tell Mac to meet us at the station pronto."

It was a fairly short ride, but the policeman did not invite conversation, and Jonathan huddled close to Inky in silence. They finally came to a halt in front of police headquarters in the neighboring town of Mendham. At the same time that Jonathan and Inky got out of the car and entered the station, a green truck roared up.

Jonathan went into a room with billboards covered with information about criminals and neighborhood activities. A policeman at a desk nodded to him, and at two men who were following close behind Jonathan. One man went straight to Inky. The pup recognized him. She jumped down from Jonathan's arms to meet him, wagged her tail, and then returned to Jonathan's side.

"Is that the dog, Mac?"

The man nodded to the policeman, "Nice work, Flannagan. That's Inky, all right."

The other man who arrived with Mac was soft-spoken and quiet, and he reminded Jonathan of his

own father. He didn't look at Inky, but kept watching Jonathan. Finally he sat down beside him.

"Hello, young man, I'm Bret Gordon. What's your name?"

Jonathan told him. Then, before he knew it, he was telling Mr. Gordon the story of Inky.

As he talked, the man called Mac examined the pup competently, thoroughly.

"Stomach okay. Pads, worn. Puncture here, but healing. Thin, not too bad. Young man, what have you fed her?"

Jonathan replied, "Milk for supper. Hamburger mixed with egg for breakfast. Good hamburger, sir. It was for my dinner."

Mac nodded approval. "Good, good. Well, Bret, unless you'd like me to fatten her up a bit, you can have her as is."

The friendly man got up, patted Inky, and then looked her over. "Okay, Mac, I'll take her along now. I have an idea."

Mac grinned broadly. "I can read your mind, Bret. She's all yours, the best one I've raised in three years. A real prizewinner. Keep her happy."

Mr. Gordon turned to Jonathan. "Come on, Jonathan, I'll give you a lift."

Outside, Mr. Gordon pointed to the green truck

and motioned Jonathan to get in the front seat. Then he opened the rear of the car which contained four cages. He carefully lifted Inky into one of these. Then he shut the cage door and jumped in front with Jonathan.

"Now Johnny, let's have a talk."

Jonathan slumped down on the seat beside his new friend. Tears gathered in his eyes. Mr. Gordon passed him a clean handkerchief, told him to blow his nose, and then to sit up and talk to him man to man. In a few minutes Jonathan felt better.

"Gosh, Mr. Gordon, you're lucky to have a dog like Inky for your very own."

Mr. Gordon shook his head. "But she isn't mine, Jonathan. Inky won't really have a master for about fourteen months. And when she does get one — well — Inky will be his eyes. You see, Jonathan, *Inky is a Seeing Eye dog*."

Jonathan began to understand then why the police had been so anxious to find Inky. Almost every child in New Jersey had heard about Seeing Eye dogs — the dogs that were trained to lead blind people. He had seen movies of these dogs training in Morristown, learning to walk in traffic and to lead their masters safely across streets.

"Jonathan, would you like to hear about Inky?"

The boy nodded eagerly, and sat back as Mr. Gordon began:

"Inky was born three months ago at the Seeing Eye breeding farm near Mendham. Mac — he's the one you just met — is our chief breeder. For years now Mac has been developing Seeing Eye dogs by careful breeding. These dogs are gentle, smart, loyal — just like Inky. Inky is one of his best pups."

Mr. Gordon then explained what had happened to Inky. A week ago Mac had taken Inky and her brothers and sisters on their last walk across country. On this walk he planned to make a final study of the puppies.

He wanted to see how they coordinated, the way they approached puppy problems, and how they solved these problems. Mac and his pups went a little bit farther than usual, deeper into the woods. It was then that Mac was ambushed by the same fellow who had stolen Jonathan's chickens.

"He robbed Mac and then picked up Inky, out of the entire litter. Said he wanted a watchdog. Poor fellow, you know, he might just have been lonely. Well anyway, that started off a state-wide dog and man hunt. All the police around here turned out, worked after hours, because Mac said Inky was such a good pup."

29

As they neared his farm, Jonathan told Mr. Gordon to turn at the sign of the 4-H clover leaf on the gatepost.

"You a member?" Mr. Gordon asked.

The boy proudly told him about his chickens and egg project. "But I guess I'll have to go back to them and wait till Dad comes home before I get my dog," he added a little sadly.

Mr. Gordon pulled up his truck outside the farmhouse, turned off the engine, and cocked his head toward the rear where Inky was riding.

"Jonathan, how would you like to borrow Inky for the next twelve months?"

Jonathan frowned. "Borrow Inky, Mr. Gordon?"

"Yes, 4-H club members raise pups for us here in northern New Jersey. We supply money for the dogs' food and veterinarian bills. And you 4-H boys and girls supply homes, love, and kindness. I am a sort of liaison man between The Seeing Eye and 4-H."

Then he explained that kennel-raised dogs aren't the same as dogs who grow up with children, in a normal home. The kennel dogs are never exposed to the sights and sounds of a home, to a baby crying, a TV or radio program, slamming doors, or the start of an automobile. They don't learn how to walk on linoleum, or to meet milkmen or postmen, or to develop affection or toleration for more than one person: their kennel master.

"I've placed a lot of puppies with boys like you, Johnny. I know you and Inky would make a good team."

Mr. Gordon got out and went around to Inky. Jonathan's mother came out on the porch just then, and Mr. Gordon went over to speak to her. Jonathan knew they would be talking about Inky.

Jonathan just sat there in the front seat, asking himself questions.

How could he give Inky up in twelve months after he'd learned to love her? How could he let her go, to walk along hot, paved city streets, leading some blind man? How could she get into harness after the freedom of a farm?

He closed his eyes and tried to imagine what it would be like to be blind. A blind man would have to use his hands to feel Inky. He could never see how beautiful she really was. He'd just use her, as a sort of machine, to get him from place to place. And she would always be dreaming of Jonathan and the farm and running free.

His mother and Mr. Gordon were standing at the car door with Inky.

"Jonathan," his mother asked him softly, "what have you decided?"

The boy looked at them both. "I don't know, Mom. I don't know how I could ever give Inky up."

"Think of it this way, Jonathan," his mother said. "I have really just borrowed you. Someday you'll grow up and leave Daddy and me. You'll make your own life because you'll want to then. It's the same way with Inky. She's born and bred to be an important dog, to help others to live again. She'll know this when the time comes. It's up to you to give her happy puppy memories."

Jonathan thought about what his mother had said for several minutes, and he saw that she was right. He knew now why he had been so proud of Inky. He turned to Mr. Gordon. "Okay, sir, I'll do it. I'll do the very best I can."

Mr. Gordon nodded. "I know you will, Jonathan. I knew it when we talked at the police station. So did Mac. That's why we're trusting you with Inky."

He handed the boy a leather collar and tag. On the tag was inscribed "The Seeing Eye, Morristown."

That was the tag which would make Inky different from every dog in town. Suddenly Jonathan felt very, very proud of the work that lay ahead for him and Inky in the next twelve months.

Work and Play

JONATHAN POUNDED THE LAST STAKE into the ground, nailed the wire fence to it, and called Inky. The puppy, roaming in the barn, came bounding to him.

"This," said Jonathan, "is your new home when I'm at school, or when Mom is too busy to have you in the house with her."

The puppy followed Jonathan into the run. It was built alongside the farmhouse, of stout wire fencing. It was twenty feet long and half as wide, with a snug doghouse filled with hay at one end. Jonathan had laid the cement foundation for the house, and the rest of the run was gravel. He placed a large pail of water in a spot at the far end of the run, which he thatched over with pine boughs for shade.

Jonathan and Inky sat down on the porch of the doghouse.

"Mr. Gordon says you can't run free all the time, Inky, especially if there is no one here to watch you."

The puppy sniffed cautiously inside her new house. She then quickly returned to Jonathan's lap. It was clear where she preferred to sit.

"You have got to be disciplined, Inky," Jonathan went on severely. "It's for your own good."

The puppy's tail wagged in agreement to any-thing he had to say, and she placed a soft muzzle against Jonathan's arm. Inky's eyes were full of merriment. She was ready for play, not discipline.

"I just want you to know all about it," Jonathan continued weakly. "Because later I have to go to church with Mom."

Then, as if her lesson had been learned, Inky bounced up and ran out of her kennel. Getting down on her front legs, yipping and tossing her head toward the woods, she began to coax Jona-than to play. Finally, unable to resist, he jumped up and was after her. The two of them were off at a run, headed toward the open pasture and the meadowlands beyond the place where old Duncan MacGregor kept his fine herd of Scotch mountain sheep.

Inky had not yet been introduced to sheep. When the boy and dog reached the crest of the long hill, they saw far below them the little patches of sheep already heavy in their new winter coats. They were grazing placidly quite a distance from the farmer's sheepcote.

Suddenly Inky caught their scent and she bounded toward them. She was too excited to heed Jonathan's call, and the boy found himself racing headlong after her. As Inky neared the animals, she began to round them up, playfully nipping their little black heels. She was barking wildly, and her tail was wagging. She was having a wonderful romp.

Just as Jonathan reached her, he saw old Mr. MacGregor appear at the top of the hillock, waving furiously, a gun in one hand. Jonathan remembered that the old man had a reputation for being a dog hater. The boy reached Inky just in time to pull her down to the ground with a flying tackle. The farmer was upon them like an angry bear.

"Get this wolf off my property!" he yelled.

"But sir, Inky's just a pup. She's only playing."

The farmer slapped his gun. "She's a sheep killer. I know the breed. Off with you both. This is my last warning. Next time I'll shoot her."

The boy hastily swept Inky into his arms and stumbled away up the hill. He looked back just once to see Mr. MacGregor sitting on a rock with his gun cocked.

Later, telling his mother about the incident, Jonathan asked, "Is there a wolf strain in Inky? She charged down the hill almost as if she really might kill those sheep. She was so excited I couldn't control her."

His mother thought about it for a while and nodded. "Perhaps deep down inside all dogs there is a hunter instinct, Johnny. Especially in dogs from northern countries, like Inky, where the wolf strain is strongest."

Then she told him one theory about domestic dogs that seemed to explain Inky's actions. She said that dogs traced their ancestry back to two lines in early history, the jackal and the wolf. The jackal fed upon carrion; the wolf was almost purely a beast of prey.

The wolf traveled in a pack and developed true

loyalty to the pack leader. This was absolutely necessary because of the harsh conditions under which they lived and hunted. The jackal, on the other hand, stayed far behind the fighting and came in as a sort of clean-up squad to feed upon anything the fighters had left.

"So the jackal was fawning and submissive when he became domesticated. He treated his man-master as his god. But the wolf was proud, and he transferred his natural allegiance to the pack leader to his man-master, and their relationship was a finer, more comradely thing."

Jonathan nodded. "So that's why Inky has to have discipline, and that's why I have to be a good leader?"

His mother smiled. "Yes, Johnny. Some dogs have no master, no home, no love, and they become real killers. But it's really because of people, usually. A killer dog is just reverting to his ancestry because he isn't cared for in a man-made society."

"Do you think Inky would really kill a sheep, Mother?"

"I don't think she would, Johnny. She's just a pup and loves to romp. I think she likes to see them jump when she nips their ankles. I can't blame her really. But that's why she needs discipline. You must learn to keep her in line."

As they left for church that morning, Inky raised her head and wailed. She was learning the first discipline of an enclosure. Jonathan worried about her all through church, and was certain she would be heartbroken when they returned. Instead, they found her snoozing peacefully in the hay.

"You see, Jonathan," his mother said, "Inky will react properly to discipline and be a happier dog for it."

Sunday marked the beginning of Inky's new routine. She ate three times a day in the kitchen from her own dish. Jonathan prepared the food himself, mixing cod-liver oil, dog meal, and meat together, and moistening it with rich, creamy milk. At breakfast, the hens laid an egg for Inky, and this was also mixed into her food. Her coat responded beautifully to the egg diet, and became more and more glossy with each daily grooming.

During her first week at the farm, Inky gained two pounds, which Jonathan faithfully recorded in his 4-H diary. The diary also noted when Inky received her distemper and hepatitis shots, and when she was checked for worms. One day Jonathan would give the diary — and Inky — back to Mr. Gordon, but there were still hundreds of pages to go, and Jonathan refused to think about the last entry in the diary.

At night, Inky slept at the foot of Jonathan's bed; and when they awoke, they did the early-morning chores together. There was generally time left for a long run in the woods before school. Then Mrs. Jones took over.

Into the kennel went Inky until household chores were finished. Then it was another walk or a trip to market in the Jones' jeep. Inky rode precariously between front and back seat, tail wagging, eyes alert for passing pedestrian dogs. These she usually yipped at, as if pleased to be riding in her mistress' car while the ordinary dogs walked.

Later she learned to sit in the jeep and to guard the vehicle while Mrs. Jones did the marketing. No one could pet Inky while she sat alone in the jeep, although the entire village of Valley View soon came to know her by name and reputation.

"That's a real Seeing Eye puppy," people would explain to their children or to town visitors. "Someday she'll be leading a blind person. Isn't it wonderful what those dogs can learn to do?"

And Inky would smile at them. She seemed to understand what they were saying, as if she too were proud of the work that was ahead of her.

Jonathan found her fairly easy to train. The Seeing Eye people didn't want him to teach her anything but the rudiments of good behavior, as they had their own system of training to be used later on. But she learned to come, to sit, and to be a real lady in her own home. She walked naturally on a leash, and during her schooling she seemed almost human in her understanding of Jonathan's commands.

But she was still very much a young, inquisitive puppy. She always tried to lure Jonathan back to the forbidden meadow and to the waiting, woolly sheep. Jonathan, remembering old MacGregor and his gun, kept Inky strictly on the Jones' property.

It was about a month after she arrived that Inky slipped away from Jonathan for the first time. Jonathan was cleaning the barn, and he did not notice her absence. Finally, when his tasks were done, he whistled for Inky. She did not appear.

Jonathan searched the woods and fields for two hours, and finally decided that there was just one place left for Inky to go. Reluctantly he turned toward the MacGregor farm, hoping desperately that the quiet afternoon air would not be shattered by the report of a rifle. Just as he reached the hilltop, he saw Inky and another large dog. They were racing merrily down the path that led from the sheep pasture. Inky was covered with burrs and mud. Behind her, tumbling in great haste, came a shaggy, surly mongrel. Jonathan had seen him often

41

skulking around town by the railroad tracks. The boy grabbed Inky by her collar and brought her to his side. The other dog continued his retreat toward the village. That, thought Jonathan, was the masterless sort of killer his mother had told him about. He felt very sorry for the dog. It might have been a good one, if someone had cared for it and trained it properly.

Inky spent the rest of the afternoon in the doghouse. No further correction was needed for Inky, sensitive to Jonathan's every mood. It was only after supper that she was allowed to come indoors, where she was studiously ignored by Jonathan and his mother. They were all sitting in front of the fireplace when they heard a car drive up. Inky rushed to the front door, growling. In a few minutes there was a heavy knock at the door:

"It's Officer Fairbarn, Mrs. Jones."

Mrs. Jones opened the door. The policeman entered, followed by old Mr. MacGregor.

"That's the other dog, all right," he snapped, pointing to Inky. "They were after my sheep this morning, Jeanie Jones, and I warned your son about it."

"Sit down, Duncan MacGregor, and mind your manners," Mrs. Jones said tartly. "Now let the officer tell us what this is all about."

42

The old Scotsman removed his cap and sat down, still peevish. He laid his gun beside him on the floor. As he sat there, Inky went toward him, tail wagging. She covered every inch of his trousers and coat with her inquisitive nose. The irate farmer sat, terrified, as if she were about to devour him, coat, pants, overshoes, and all.

"Duncan MacGregor says Inky and another dog — we've found him in town — were chasing his sheep today. One sheep was badly bitten in the flank. We think the big dog meant business. There were pieces of wool in his back teeth."

Officer Fairbarn paused and looked at Inky. "The Animal Rescue League has him now. And Duncan here wants me to take Inky —"

Jonathan jumped to his feet, but his mother restrained him. She spoke in a very calm voice.

"I can understand how you feel, Duncan. You have a very fine herd of sheep."

"Aye, and I intend to keep them that way."

"But I can't understand why a grown man like you is so afraid of dogs that you have to keep a gun at your side."

"Who says I'm afraid, Jeannie Jones? I'm protecting my sheep from dogs that come down on the fold like wolves in the night."

Mrs. Jones pointed to Inky. "All right, let's see

you reach out and pet Inky, if you aren't afraid of dogs. She's gentle and harmless."

There was a long silence. Inky seated herself next to the farmer, on the hearth. Her head was turned toward him, muzzle bracketed between her paws. She wagged her tail ever so slightly, but she didn't move. The farmer looked from Mrs. Jones to her son to the policeman. No one offered assistance.

Finally, cowed by the stony silence, he reached out a gnarled, timid hand. Inky arose quietly, walked over to him, and put her head on his lap. She remained motionless until Duncan MacGregor worked up enough courage to stroke her head. It was an awkward motion, as if he hadn't been gentle and loving in many years. Inky seemed to like the smell of him, and she almost seemed to sense his fear and longing. They remained like that for several minutes, until the old man said grudgingly, "She does seem gentle enough now, doesn't she?"

"You know, Duncan, Inky's no ordinary pup. She's going to be a Seeing Eye dog when she grows up."

"And what may that be, Jeannie Jones?"

The farmer made no effort now to dislodge Inky's head from his lap. Instead, his fingers gently stroked her ears. He was no longer afraid.

"They are dog guides, trained to lead the blind," explained Officer Fairbarn. "That's why I found it so hard to believe that Inky is a sheep killer. She's mischievous perhaps, but not a killer."

The farmer looked down at the dog curiously. "You mean they actually train these animals to lead blind people?"

Jonathan spoke up. "Well, sir, that's what Inky will be doing in about a year from now, if nothing happens to her."

The farmer laughed, "All right, young Jonathan Jones, you win. Perhaps if you bring her up to the house on a leash, we can teach her how to treat my sheep."

When they had left, Mrs. Jones hugged her son and Inky, all in one squash. "Johnny, when we write Dad tonight, we must tell him what a smart pup we have. How he'd have loved to see Inky win over that old Scotsman!"

When Mr. Gordon came by on his next visit, Jonathan told him the story, and his friend was interested. "Let's take Inky up there on a leash, as MacGregor suggested. We've got to know, one way or another, just how fond Inky is of sheep!"

On their way up to the farmer's field, Mr. Gordon explained:

"Jonathan, you know we do have some trouble

with pups that get off to a wrong start with live-stock. They start chasing chickens, for instance, just for the fun of seeing the feathers fly. Then one day they nip a little deeper, taste blood, and you have a potential chicken killer. They've got to be corrected in time, before it gets to be a habit."

The boy nodded. "But Mr. Gordon, Inky never bothers our farm animals."

"That's true. She knows they belong to you and it's her job to protect them. Also, your stock doesn't roam like sheep in untidy groups all over the valley. Years and years ago, German shepherds tended sheep. Maybe that age-old instinct to round them up gets hold of Inky."

As they neared the sheep, Inky began to quiver. Mr. Gordon took her lead and jerked it short. "No, Inky, no," he said quietly. "These are our friends."

After several attempts to reach the sheep, Inky gradually quieted down. Mr. Gordon patted her head gently. "Good dog, Inky. Good dog."

The sheep watched them approach warily, and the visitors stood by until the animals became accustomed to their presence. Then they approached, with Inky held close on a slip chain. The dog sniffed the sheep, and when they did not run, she looked up at Jonathan and Mr. Gordon and yawned.

"She's telling us how dull they suddenly are," said Mr. Gordon. "You see, it *was* just puppy mischief after all. Now that she's met them properly, I doubt we'll have any more trouble."

Duncan MacGregor joined them. He no longer carried a gun, and his blue eyes seemed to have a merry twinkle in them. Jonathan's mouth dropped open when he saw the farmer stoop down and pat Inky.

"That's a good wee doggy," he said. "You see, we're old neighbors."

"Mr. MacGregor," Mr. Gordon said, "some of my friends keep a black angus with their sheep. They tell me it's purely psychological, like keeping a scarecrow in your corn patch. But the angus looks just tough enough to take on any marauder."

The farmer nodded. "But I've an even better idea. Come along." He led them to his barn. Inky, racing ahead, found it first. Nestled in the hay, sound asleep, was a little brown and white puff of fur. It stretched, yawned, looked up, and touched noses with Inky.

"Meet Glamis," Mr. MacGregor chuckled softly. "She's a fine Shetland sheep puppy. She'll be all I'll need to watch the lambs."

A Round-Robin Letter

"Inky, you are a very fine dog, but —"
Mrs. Jones addressed herself partly to Inky, partly
to Jonathan. It was a way she had of talking when
the three of them were together, as if Inky under-
stood every word she said.

"But what, Mom?" Jonathan knew his mother
was starting on one of her indirect lectures. Inky
cocked her head too, waiting.

"But how can we teach her not to jump up on me
when I have just put on a clean dress and she has
been out in the mud?"

She held out her skirt. "See, paw marks right up
to my shoulders. At least we know she's growing."

48

Jonathan suggested that his mother wear an apron, but Mrs. Jones refused to accept the idea. "No, Johnny, there must be some way to train her. Next time Mr. Gordon comes by, ask him."

Mr. Gordon, in a simple demonstration, showed both Jonathan and his mother how to break Inky of her bad habit.

"Watch me," he said, approaching Inky's kennel with a show of friendliness. "Hello, Inky, you beautiful dog." His voice was soft and wooing, and as soon as she was free, Inky jumped up on Mr. Gordon's jacket. Immediately he stepped firmly on her rear foot, jerking her down at the same time with a pull at her collar. "Down girl, down."

Inky's feelings were hurt. She turned to Jonathan for comfort, jumping boisterously on his shirt. He copied Mr. Gordon's example, stepping on Inky's rear foot, pulling down with her collar, giving the command, "Down, girl." Inky was beginning to realize that she was making a mistake. Her third try, on Mrs. Jones, resulted in final comprehension. Only a few times after that did she forget herself and jump up. Within a week she was completely corrected.

"Of course," Mr. Gordon told Jonathan, "you aren't the only 4-H member with problems! I'd like

49

to take you around to some of the other homes, but they are all so scattered. Tell you what I can do, though. The children have started a round-robin letter that helps them all in working out problems. If they can't solve them, they write for help; if they know the answers, they tell everyone else about it in the letter. I'll put you on the mailing list, Jonathan."

When the letter arrived, Jonathan realized that he and Inky were really partners in a hard-working organization. From the past, he knew that the 4-H Club to which he belonged was part of the United States Department of Agriculture's extension service. The 4-H program encouraged children to learn about farming and homemaking, but it also stressed good citizenship and community service. And that was how The Seeing Eye and the 4-H clubs in New Jersey had joined hands. The Seeing Eye wanted puppies raised in homes near their famous training school at Morristown; 4-H members could give the pups these homes and, indirectly, help all the blind people who needed good dogs. The Seeing Eye supplied the money to meet the puppy-raising expenses.

The round-robin letter, Jonathan saw, was written by many kinds of people whose one interest was in raising good, strong Seeing Eye pups.

The letter started out with a note of caution from a veterinarian. He asked all 4-H members to be careful during the autumn months. "Be sure your dog receives no sudden exposure to the changes in weather," he wrote. "We are starting to have rainy and windy days. Make certain your dog has a dry place to sleep."

Another letter told Jonathan how much The Seeing Eye program meant to people who bred dogs for a living. A man who raised championship boxers notified 4-H members to contact Bret Gordon on his next stop at any of their homes. "We've just had a wonderful litter, and if there is a Seeing Eye pup among them, I want Bret Gordon to come over and pick it out. Of course the pups themselves can't see yet, but I hope someday one of them will see for someone without eyes."

A 4-H leader reported on rabbits: "As you may know, we have a Seeing Eye puppy named Dorothy — Dot for short. She gets pretty excited sometimes over my son's rabbits, but she is getting more and more used to them. I think it helps in the dogs' early training if they become used to other animals and don't chase them."

Someone at The Seeing Eye school itself had endorsed the leader's remarks: "You are absolutely right. We sent a German shepherd out with her blind mistress, fully trained, we thought, for any emergency. But the shepherd had never seen squirrels before, and her mistress had to cross a squirrel-infested park to work every day. We had to send a special man out to break her of the squirrel-chasing habit!"

A ten-year-old girl, who was also the club secretary, wrote that she had built two doghouses, one for her own boxer, Warren; the other for her Seeing Eye pup, Bobs. "Don't make the mistake I did of building two houses, because my two dogs insist on sleeping together. When Bobs has gone to The Seeing Eye, I'll bet Warren will miss her!"

A letter from a farm boy interested Jonathan, thinking back on his own recent adventure with Inky. The boy wrote:

"It wasn't long before Manly discovered that it was great sport to chase chickens. He did this three times, and each time was severely scolded and tied up. The fourth time, however, he not only caught a chicken, but killed it too. This was too much. Having emptied a can of red pepper on the dead chicken, we tied it around his neck. When I came home from school, the chicken was gone and not a trace of feathers or bone was to be found. As far as we could figure, he had pulled off the chicken, sampled it, and not liking the taste, buried it. Since then he has not bothered a chicken, rabbit, or cat."

The red-pepper solution also worked in the case of Lois, who liked to get into garbage cans. Her young mistress reported: "Red pepper helped me with Lois too. She started to take the garbage out of the can every night. As a remedy, I sprinkled red pepper over the garbage. Needless to say, she doesn't do it any more."

A fourteen-year-old girl asked for help with her Labrador retriever, Russ: "Russ has trouble getting used to the change in time. His stomach still runs on Daylight Saving Time. Every morning, an hour early, he comes and licks my face to wake me up."

"My dog's name is Jo," wrote another member. "I got her when she was seven months old. She was very shy and nervous. If you spoke to her harshly, she would crawl as though she had been mistreated. Mr. Gordon told us to play with her a lot, even roughly, so she would stop being shy. This worked in her case. She has gotten over being shy and is very affectionate."

There was also an item about a puppy named Willis: "One day I noticed Willis had a lump on his jaw, so I took him to the vet. It was an abscess, and Willis had to stay at the vet's for a week. He is all right now, is forty inches long, twenty-two high, and weighs sixty-five pounds. But always watch out for lumps. The vet said they may develop into something dangerous if not checked in time."

There were also vital statistics on pups that interested Jonathan: "Alvy is a very mischievous shepherd. She has gained eight pounds in two months. She is also growing in height, and we think she is growing out of the puppy stage. She barks now instead of yipping. We all enjoy watching her grow up, especially Mom."

Another problem was posed by an overly affectionate uncle: "My uncle Otto lives near us, and my aunt won't let him have a dog, so he comes over while I am at school and plays with Weezy, my boxer. He brings her bones, and sometimes I think she likes him better than she does me. This is hard, because I have to scold her when she is bad, and Uncle Otto just pets her."

One 4-H member suggested that his dog, Menise, might make a better police dog than Seeing Eye dog: "Her technique of bringing people down to earth is really superb. When someone gets a head start playing cops and robbers, Menise will tear after him. She dashes between his legs and sends him flying. She is also a good detective. I once caught her trailing our Siamese cat, Ching, staying an even five paces behind him. If Ching stopped and turned around, Menise would halt and scratch a flea or sniff industriously at some passing insect."

The last letter was written by a girl who had raised three dogs for the Seeing Eye program: a Labrador retriever, a Norwegian elkhound, and a German shepherd. She was now waiting for Mr. Gordon to bring her a fourth.

"One of the first questions my friends ask after Mr. Gordon comes to take the pups away is, 'Don't you miss them?' Yes, I miss them, but I know they aren't mine to begin with and that they're going to good homes. Many members of the 4-H say the new puppies they get take the grown dogs' place. This is not the case for me. Sweet, cuddly Mary, the elkhound, could never take the place of big, bouncy Ruth, the retriever; nor could Dunc, who loves a game, ever take the place of Mary."

After reading the comments and problems of his unseen friends, Jonathan added his own bit of information to the round-robin letter:

"My Seeing Eye pup Inky no longer jumps on

Mother's clean dresses. If your dog does this, just step firmly on her back toes, pull her collar, and say, 'Down, girl.' Or, if it's a male, say 'Down, boy.'"

He had just finished writing when he heard a loud wail of protest from his mother in the kitchen.

"Inky, no girl, go away, far, far away. Out of my kitchen!"

Jonathan reached the kitchen in time to see his mother slam the door in the face of his beloved puppy.

"Johnny, Inky has just met a skunk!"

That night Jonathan added still another footnote to the round-robin letter:

"If your dog should meet up with a skunk, you wash her in tomato juice. Rub the juice into her fur, and leave it on for a few minutes. Then rinse it off well, with water. You'll probably need lots of tomato juice, but this method really works. Poor Inky seemed to like the skunk smell, and couldn't understand why we were so upset. We were thinking of changing her name from Inky to Stinky."

A Visit to the Kennels

It was several weeks after Inky's misadventure with the skunk that the green Seeing Eye truck drove up to the Jones farm. Jonathan and Inky had just finished watering the horses.

"Hello, Jonathan," Mr. Gordon called out to him. "Like to go on a trip up to the breeding farm with me? Mac wants to see how Inky is doing."

At the sight of the boy's worried frown, The Seeing Eye man laughed.

"It's nothing serious, Johnny. Mac's very much interested in Inky. She's his special pup. And this is a special invitation. Very few outside dogs or people are ever invited to the farm."

Immediately reassured, Jonathan and Inky bounded for the truck. The horses, so hastily deserted, watched curiously from their corral, and were unable to explain anything to Mrs. Jones when she returned shortly from marketing.

The Seeing Eye breeding farm was about ten miles north of Jonathan's farm, in the hills. There, on a hundred-acre tract surrounded by woods and streams, live the fathers and mothers of the pups that grow up to lead the blind.

There are no signs pointing to the farm, and Mr. Gordon explained that the farm dogs require utmost privacy.

"We used to raise pups down at the school in Whippany, where the dogs are trained for their guide work. But we find the pups are better protected from diseases up here. It's quiet, too."

The truck maneuvered up a dirt road, past a white farmhouse, and into a driveway behind a large, two-storied barn. They parked in the driveway and got out.

Far beyond the barn were rows and rows of fenced runs. Jonathan saw great black and tan dogs sitting on the tops of some of the doghouses in the runs. Others were pacing back and forth. Still others were playing and wrestling.

From the barn itself, Jonathan heard the sharp yips of puppies. He couldn't remember just when it was that Inky's own puppy bark had changed to that full-throated bay she now possessed. He looked down at her, standing silently at his side. Her head was cocked toward the kennels, as if remembering that this had once been her home.

Mac was coming toward them from the barn. He was a tall young man with an easy walk, and he smiled broadly at the sight of Inky. His quick, trained eyes sized up the half-grown pup at Jonathan's side. He nodded approvingly:

"Jonathan, that's a magnificent pup you're raising."

The boy patted Inky's head. "You gave her a good start, sir."

Mr. Gordon intervened. "Let's check her out, Mac."

He took the pup from Jonathan and walked her up and down fast along the gravel path. She seemed to please Mac, who watched her every movement.

"Strong hindquarters, Bret. Nice size. Graceful. Alert. Handles her body well."

He continued his appraisal, half to himself. "Good feet, too. Well up on her pasterns. Nice rigid back."

Mac made a sudden lurch toward Inky, as if to strike her with his open hand. There was no reaction except extreme wariness in the dog's eyes.

"Good dog." Mac patted her with hands that knowingly felt her muscles, her coat, the conformation of her chest.

"One of her sisters was absolutely terrified of sudden noises. We couldn't use her. She was just too timid. Beautiful dog, too."

Then he turned to Jonathan. "Like to see where Inky was born?"

The boy nodded eagerly.

Mac took Inky by her lead and put her back in the truck. "We don't want our dogs here to have any contact with canine visitors. There's a fortune in dog talent here in the kennels and up in the pup nursery in the barn."

The three went toward a building which Mac described as the clinic. Upon entering, they washed their shoes in an antiseptic solution. They entered an immaculate office where the dogs were treated for ailments and given their shots. The clinic was equipped with a medical library, scales, formula bottles, even dental tools. "We clean the mothers' teeth once or twice a year," Mac said. "And believe me, they feel the same way most of us do about going to the dentist."

The dogs were groomed daily and their ears cleaned thoroughly. All food was scientifically mixed and weighed with special formulae that developed strong bones and teeth. Careful charts were kept of the pups, including their weight.

"We stand on the scale with the pup in our arms," Mac explained. "When our own weight is subtracted, the rest is pup."

Mac pointed to a sign at the far side of the room which said "Keep out." That, he said, was the maternity ward where Inky and hundreds of other puppies had been born.

"We can't show you the mothers, because we like to keep them isolated. There are two behind there now, in large comfortable stalls filled with paper. We take the mothers out about six times a day for exercise, and to clean the maternity stall. Later, when the pups are steadier on their legs, they all go out in good weather in outdoor runs."

Jonathan learned that only German shepherds were bred at the farm, although the Seeing Eye uses other breeds such as boxers, Labrador retrievers, and other selected individuals.

"You see," Mac told him, "we are trying to control our breeding. In order to do this, we want to know all there is to know about the background

62

of the father and mother, of their fathers and mothers, as far back as we can go. In this way we know how to breed out weak spots that are the result of heredity. For instance, we discovered that a beautiful mother, perfect in every other way, transmitted a tendency toward car sickness to her pups. We had to work that problem out. Eventually we hope to breed perfect pups all the time."

"And now," he suggested, "let's go out to the kennels and meet Inky's parents."

They left the maternity ward and went out to the long lines of kennels. In one large compound, Mac pointed to two beautifully marked German shepherds. One was much larger than his mate, jet black in color, with just a faint hint of brown over eyes and under tail. His mate, smaller, daintier, was flecked with brown splotches, in much the same way that Inky was marked. They were playing happily together, and suddenly seeing Mac, they raced for the fence.

Their bark of greeting set off the entire row of some twenty-four dogs, and for a minute no one could speak for the bedlam. Finally it subsided as they concentrated on the two magnificent animals before them.

"Jonathan," said Mac, "meet Hana and Bruce,

Inky's parents. Bruce here is a descendant of one of the first dog guides, and his ancestors worked with German soldiers blinded in the First World War. Hana, on the other hand, is from sound, working American stock."

Jonathan reached his hand through the fence and felt a welcoming nuzzling of two cold and inquisitive noses. He wondered if they recognized the smell of their daughter, Inky.

"This pair won't ever be dog guides, of course," Mac told him. "But their pups are out all over, leading the blind. There are more than twelve hundred Seeing Eye dogs working in harness right now."

Jonathan gave in to temptation and shyly asked a question that had been bothering him ever since he arrived:

"Which ones do you think are the happiest dogs, the ones here on the farm, or their pups, on the outside?"

Mr. Gordon and Mac exchanged smiles. Mac finally replied, thoughtfully, "Jonathan, many sentimental people imagine that dog guides are unhappy when they see them working, intently, on the street. But Seeing Eye dogs enjoy this work because they are intelligent dogs. The more an intelligent dog can learn, the happier he is."

Mr. Gordon broke in: "Johnny, you've known people who just keep their dogs tied up, for their entire lives, and never go near them. Watchdogs, they call them. Then they wonder why the dog barks and the neighbors complain. That dog is being treated like an imbecile, and he's bound to get neurotic."

"And most dogs are like people," Mac continued. "They like to be useful. For a Seeing Eye dog, the reward is double. He helps his sightless master achieve independence and companionship. And the dog himself realizes the ambition of all dogs. That ambition is to be with his master, day and night."

Then they told him about a very remarkable blind man named Morris Frank, who brought the first Seeing Eye dog to the United States in 1928. Mr. Frank had to prove that a dog could lead a blind man through American traffic; later he had to lead the fight to have dog guides accepted in restaurants and on public conveyances. Everyone today knows how Morris Frank succeeded. But Mac went on to tell Jonathan something about Mr. Frank's dogs, all of them named Buddy, after the first Buddy who pioneered guide-dog work in this country.

"At home, the present Buddy is a real house pet," Mac said. "She's just like Inky. She loves to coax the family to play with her rubber ball. She pays no attention to sighted people, but even when she is out of harness in the house, she keeps a watchful eye on Morris Frank when he's in the room. It's as if she has to know where he is and what he's doing every minute. She goes crazy when he swims away from her in a pool and she can't get to him."

Mac told Jonathan that Buddy even has her own group of dog friends with whom she romps in the neighborhood, "on her own time."

"There's one St. Bernard who is terribly attached to her," Mac recalled. "Whenever she appears, he joins up with Buddy and they dash off together. This also happens, unfortunately, when Buddy is in harness. The St. Bernard will come up to Buddy and forcibly try to free her from her harness. They often have a terrible scuffle, right on Main Street, Mr. Frank and that St. Bernard. Buddy tries to ignore her affectionate friend, but this is often quite difficult because of his size and devotion.

"However, when Morris Frank gets away from the village, and on his way to work at his insurance office in Morristown, Buddy is a different dog.

"It's a miracle to watch a well-trained dog and master work as a team," Mac continued. "If a friend joins Mr. Frank on the street and takes his arm, Buddy automatically drops behind on rein. But when her master starts out with that long rapid gait of his for the barbershop or a business call, Buddy steps out briskly, taking in stride traffic, overhanging awnings, and silly old ladies who want to stop and pat her."

Eventually they said good-bye to Hana and Bruce, and retraced their steps toward the barn where Jonathan had heard the puppy yelps.

"Now we'll show you some career babies, Jonathan."

Mr. Gordon pointed to a long wooden ramp leading to the second story of the barn. "Mac will send down a group of puppies for me to look at, because I'll be taking them to 4-H homes in a few weeks. I want to know all about them."

Mac disappeared behind the barn, and in a few minutes a trap door opened from the ramp, and seven little bundles of black and tan fur started tentatively down the steep, cleated ramp.

"Hi, pup-pups," Mr. Gordon called, and hearing a voice at the other end, they began a faster descent.

Once on the ground, they advanced in a wave of wiggles toward Jonathan and his friend.

"These are the K kids," said Mac, joining them. "All their names will start with K. It's an easy way to keep track of litters as we place them."

Jonathan tried to think of K names: "Karen, Kathy, Kitty, Ken —"

He ran out of names. Mac added: "Kiji, Krishna, Kuri. We don't care what part of the world the names come from, as long as they are short and sharp and the pups get to recognize them in a day or so. Of course, some of the 4-H kids insist on long, romantic names, but eventually they all get shortened."

From the truck, Inky was now making cooing noises at the little band of pups. The pups reacted immediately and bounced toward their canine friend's extended black nose. They clambered up the side of the truck and fell back unsteadily, as their little legs gave way against the slippery side.

"Wait till you're ten weeks old, pup-pups," Mac Gordon told them. "You'll be riding off in this very truck, and probably you'll be complaining loudly. You all do! Or else you get carsick. I don't know which is worse."

Then Mac and Mr. Gordon began to study the little balls of activated fur. Mac pointed out a pup which he thought had good qualities.

"She's a lot like Inky — fearless, placid, alert. Excellent hindquarters. That's the real working part of the dog guide, Jonathan."

Mac selected another pup. "I'm afraid she'll be overly shy. Noises bother her. And this little fellow —"

He held up a smaller pup that whimpered when he touched it.

"Bad coordination, a real tanglefoot. Same with the female of the same parents two litters ago. But I think we can plan on at least four good ones. A couple will need training in certain lines, Bret. For example, this little yacker here."

He pointed out a small and noisy pup who had been yipping from the moment she set foot on the ground, mostly at the truck tires.

"Like a lot of women. Yak, yak, yak. And she hasn't got a thing to say."

Mac picked up the talkative pup in his arms, spoke to her gently, and she immediately quieted down. "Just needs a little individual attention, Bret. Find her a quiet home with maybe one firm, older boy who is affectionate with dogs. That just may do it."

The two men then discussed the 4-H homes where the puppies would be placed for a year. They would be scattered all over New Jersey, on

farms, in university towns, in back mountains, at resort lakes.

"But all these 4-H homes are like the Jones farm," Mr. Gordon grinned. "Every kid loves his pup, and he gives it food, exercise, discipline, and love. Right, Johnny?"

As they climbed back in the truck and backed out to the dirt road, Inky threw back her head and bayed like a wolf toward the long kennels where her parents lived.

"She must be saying good-bye now, for good," Mr. Gordon said.

And from the cages at the far end of the farm came an answering call. Jonathan saw Inky's mother, perched on the roof of her kennel, watching the truck as it drove off, and howling. It was a sad, lonesome sound. Jonathan thought of snow and dark forests and wild, yellow eyes. Inky and her parents had come a long way in civilization from those faraway ancestors, but Mac still hadn't bred the wolf call out of their memories.

"Intelligent Disobedience"

HARVESTTIME ON THE FARM always meant the arrival of Uncle Jim Sutter from south Jersey. Uncle Jim had been coming to help with the crops ever since Jonathan could remember. It was a busy time of year, with the hay to get in, vegetables and fruit to put up, and the corn to stack in orderly pyramids in the lower field. There were apples to store in the root cellar, walnuts to gather for the holidays ahead, onions to dry, and of course the fun of rooting out pumpkins among the corn and saving the biggest for Halloween.

Uncle Jim and Jonathan were out in the orchard on a bright autumn morning when Jonathan's mother called from the farmhouse. The mailman had just been along, and she held up a postcard.

"Hey, Johnny, surprise, surprise!"

The boy tossed an apple into the basket he'd been filling and ran to his mother. At first he thought it might be word about his father, but the card Mrs. Jones held up was not from Korea.

"We're invited to a picnic," she told him, handing him a postcard signed with a paw mark, from The Seeing Eye. The Jones family was invited to a picnic on the grounds of the famous Seeing Eye school itself. Here they would meet other 4-H families who raised dogs for the program, and they would see some of the grown dogs actually working with their blind masters.

"Oh Mom, can we go?"

"Of course we can, Jonathan. Uncle Jim and Inky can manage the farm for just one day. We'll jump into the jeep and take off. We both need a change."

On the day of the picnic, Jonathan and his mother drove down from the hills into the busy town of Morristown, four miles from Seeing Eye headquarters. In this town the actual instruction of both dog and blind master takes place.

"Remember your history, Jonathan? Morristown is where General Washington spent two bitter winters with his ragged army in 1778 and 1779. Along these very streets marched the French reinforcements sent to help —"

Just as they rounded the Morristown square, the history lesson came to an abrupt end. Jonathan, nearly falling out of the jeep, pointed to a crowded street corner where a man and dog waited for light signals to change. The man was blindfolded; the dog was in a stiff, U-shaped leather harness.

"Look, Mom, a Seeing Eye dog, working!"

Mrs. Jones pulled the jeep over to the curb, and they watched the man and dog move on the green light to the opposite side of the street. When they reached the safety of the curb, the blindfolded man

reached down and patted the dog encouragingly. Then they continued on through the crowds, the dog on the left, taking his master through shoppers, around low-hanging store awnings, through a revolving door into a department store.

"Mother," Jonathan exploded. "How does the dog know when the light turns green? Or when an awning is too low for a man to walk under? How?"

Mrs. Jones shook her head. "It's training, wonderful training. That man was obviously one of the teachers. You saw how patient and gentle he was at the crossing."

They drove on, along tree-shaded streets, toward

the village of Whippany, where The Seeing Eye school is located. Headquarters is a gracious mansion, high on a hilltop, away from traffic noises. The mansion itself houses the blind students who come from all over the United States and its territories to obtain their dog guides. In the large, airy kennels and runs at the foot of the hill live the dogs themselves.

Jonathan and his mother had just reached the kennels when they heard Mr. Gordon's familiar voice: "Park it over here, Mrs. Jones. We're just starting a dog tour."

On the tour was an excited group of children and parents. They introduced themselves informally as they walked along behind Mr. Gordon.

One of the girls, a little older then Jonathan, had raised five dogs for the program. Another boy, slightly younger than Jonathan, confided that he was having trouble with his Elfie.

"She chews up Dad's shoes and then buries them."

They approached a large exercise pen where some twenty dogs were sunning and romping. They were all beautiful German shepherds, completely at ease with one another. Sometimes two would come together in what looked like a graceful dog dance, poised on hind legs, muzzles together. It was obvious that they were all friends.

In another pen, six or eight boxers were relaxing. These dogs did not seem to Jonathan to have the graceful abandon the shepherds had. They were stiff and muscular, but with fine coordination, a little given to clowning. The boy also noticed a few steel-gray Norwegian elkhounds, some Siberian huskies, and an airdale.

"Each dog has his own peculiarities," Mr. Gordon told them. "It's up to the trainer to study his dog and train him accordingly."

"And now," he added, "let's go on into the doghouse."

They entered a spotless room with light green tiled walls, steel bars, concrete floors, and a fan that ventilated bright, airy pens. Mr. Gordon said the floors were heated in winter with steam pipes that automatically kept the temperature at sixty degrees.

"No cold feet for our dogs," he laughed.

Two dogs were assigned to each pen. This developed a sort of dog friendship between them, and they also provided each other with companionship. There were some sixteen pens, eight on each side of a large middle aisle.

The kitchen area was immaculate. There were

lines of stainless-steel sinks where live steam spouted out to sterilize the dog pans. The dogs ate well. Mr. Gordon said that over thirty tons of horse-meat, suet, and liver was fed to them every year.

There was also an infirmary where dogs were placed "in solitary" in case they contracted distemper or other contagious diseases. They were examined weekly. If worms were found, the dogs went into special worming pens; fleas were taken care of in roomy tubs in the grooming section. Here the dogs were also brushed and curried, and had their ears cleaned.

At the end of the kennel tour, Mr. Gordon led them to a grassy expanse where box lunches were distributed, and the group sat down to talk about their dog problems. Just then a familiar green truck drove up. A tall, serious man alighted and went around to open the rear, which contained several German shepherds. They came bounding out, sniffed in the general direction of food and picnickers, and obeyed a quick command to sit.

"Hans, come on over and talk to the kids," Bret Gordon called to him. "And bring one of your dogs. I think they'd like to know how you train them."

Hans selected a particularly handsome shepherd and turned the others over to a kennel man. As he approached the group, Jonathan heard a suppressed squeal behind him. It was the girl who had raised five dogs.

"I know it's Happy," he heard her whisper to her mother. "Isn't he wonderful? Will he remember me?"

Bret Gordon caught her eye and motioned her to be quiet. But his subtle nod indicated that this was indeed Happy, now in training. Jonathan wondered how he would have acted if it had been Inky.

"Hans," Mr. Gordon exclaimed, "is one of our veteran trainers. He's been with The Seeing Eye for about twenty years. It takes from three to five years to train a trainer. They have to love and understand dogs, and they must also study animal psychology, human nature, and of course the training techniques of The Seeing Eye school. So you can see how valuable they are."

"Yes, children," Hans added, in a slightly foreign accent, "and you can't have flat feet if you want to learn my job. I wear out two pairs of thick crepe-soled shoes a year walking an average of ten miles a day. But it's always worth it, isn't it, Happy?"

The dog wagged his tail and nudged his trainer. Almost absent-mindedly, Hans dropped the un-lighted pipe he was carrying. He paid no attention to it, but the alert brown eyes of his companion hadn't missed the action.

The dog arose without command, picked up the pipe, and circled the trainer. Then he sat as Hans turned and felt for his pipe. He was rewarded by a pat and "Good boy, Happy."

"You can all probably guess why we teach them that trick," Hans spoke to his audience now. "Often a blind person may drop an object, sometimes without knowing it. The dog automatically retrieves it. They are taught to pick up metal, wood, and leather objects."

Then Hans explained very simply how The Seeing Eye dogs are trained for their guide work.

"When you have raised your dogs and they reach us," he began, "they go into classes of eight to a trainer. The instructor trains, feeds, and grooms them. They are his 'string' for three months."

The girl behind Jonathan raised her hand: "Please, sir, how long does it take them to forget us?"

Hans smiled at her, and Happy, sitting at his side, was not alerted by a once familiar voice. "Well, with boxers, it's almost overnight. They're real, lovable extroverts. With some shepherds and others it takes a little longer. Some may never quite forget, but let's say that their allegiance has been transferred from you — to me."

He added, "And of course there remains the

dog's final transfer of not only loyalty but love from trainer to blind master. Blind students tell me that it sometimes takes days for the dog to realize that he must forget his trainer and help his new master along the road to self-sufficiency. When the dog finally realizes this, a wonderful love and teamwork develops that never fails to make me realize how worthwhile all these months of training have been."

Then Hans told the children something about this training. The dog guides are taught to guide from the left, in order to be free to see and to protect. They are taught five commands: come, sit, down, rest, and fetch.

"Now this is the hard part to explain," Hans continued. "We select dogs because of their willingness to work and to learn. We teach them to use their own judgment when it is absolutely necessary for the safety of their master. We call this *intelligent disobedience*."

He told them a story to illustrate what he meant. An alert dog guide had been ordered forward by his mistress. Directly ahead of them was a crane, engaged in construction work. Suddenly the crane ripped loose from its pivot and began to swing toward the dog's mistress. The dog knew she couldn't see it coming, and within seconds it would have struck her down. He jumped up on his mistress and knocked her to the ground just as the crane swung over her.

"That's what I mean by intelligent disobedience."

Another hand went up. "How do the dogs know where they are going?"

"The dog guide doesn't take his master to a destination without being told where to go," Hans explained. "The blind man has a mental picture of where he's going. He directs his guide by three commands: right, left, and forward. It's up to the dog to get him there."

The same voice persisted: "But if a blind man can't see, how does he know where he is going?"

Hans smiled. "When the Lord took away the blind man's sight, he sharpened other faculties, such as memory, hearing, and a sense of direction. Our man memorized how many blocks to go right, how many to go left, and he's off. In a strange city, he asks directions; in a familiar home town, he soon learns locations. It's his dog who looks out for puddles and open manholes and empty elevator shafts."

Jonathan could resist it no longer. His own hand shot up. "Please, sir, how do you train dogs to watch for those things, and also for traffic lights and low awnings and things like that?"

"Young man, now you're getting to the heart of the training technique."

And he slowly explained what he meant.

"The purpose of The Seeing Eye dog, among other things," he said, "is to indicate changes of levels to his master. He does this by stopping at curbs, going around obstacles, preventing blind people from bumping their heads on low-hanging objects. He learns to do this by association. In learning through association, he also learns what the old German word 'phui' means.

"To a dog, 'phui' means that something is to be avoided or the trainer gets hurt; 'phui' means that something he has just done is bad and is not to be repeated. If he continues to bring forth 'phuis' from his trainer, he is corrected; otherwise he hears those wonderfully sweet words, 'Good dog.' Thus he learns to watch for 'phuis': low awnings, moving cars, running cats."

"Now let's take Happy here," Hans continued. "He's just about learned that I am at the other end of the lead, and that I will be hurt unless he watches his 'phuis.' Now watch us."

The trainer picked up Happy's U-shaped leather harness and ordered him forward. The dog rose and walked at a brisk pace toward two parked cars in the driveway. The vocal command, "Forward," led him straight toward the narrow space between the cars. The space was large enough for Happy to walk through; his trainer would obviously bump himself headlong into one of the vehicles. For a second on the approach, Happy seemed to pause, perplexed, but then he continued as commanded. Hans bumped into the cars and immediately spit out the word "Phui." He carefully jerked Happy's lead, hit the side of the car, and said "Phui" once more. Something seemed to begin to percolate in the dog's mind. The audience could almost see him puzzling the situation out to a logical end. When Hans repeated the performance, Happy stopped at the two cars and refused to go forward on command. He had learned his lesson. He received his reward: "Good boy!" and a pat on the head.

"You see, children, that's how it works," Hans said. "Our dogs learn to watch for potential dangers and to avoid them by intelligent disobedience."

"And now," he continued, "about those traffic lights. As far as we know, a dog is color-blind and cannot read the lights. However, there seem to be a great number of sighted people who either can't read lights or don't care what hits them. I've seen a good dog guide wait for the lights to change while a jaywalker walked right out in front of him, as if deliberately setting a bad example. I think most blind people with dogs are safer in traffic than sighted people. But to get back to those lights —"

Hans seemed to be searching for the right words. "Here again we have the association of ideas. When the light turns green for the blind man at the curb, the car coming up to the intersection stops on the red light. The trainer touches the stopped car, pats it to show it won't hurt him, and says, 'Good dog.' The dog eventually gets to know that when traffic stops in one direction, it's time for him to move. But this takes months of training and work."

The instructor then told them something about the relationship of the blind man to his dog. He said it takes at least a month at the school for the blind student to learn to use his dog guide. He must be taught how to direct the dog and how to interpret the sign language that comes through the U-shaped harness handle held lightly in the left hand. Instructors first take the role of the dogs, to better teach the blind these first few lessons. They also teach them how to feed and care for their guides.

The blind master directs the dog by oral signals. The signals that come to the man from his dog through the harness warn him of everything that is likely to interfere with his safe progress. This almost perfect communication between the two permits man and dog to work at a pace which is more rapid than that of the average pedestrian. Upon arriving at the street crossings, the dog guides his master to the edge of the curb. Here he stops. The master finds the edge immediately with his toe, and then gives the dog a command for the direction in which he wishes to go. The dog, on the other hand, will not cross unless he knows it is absolutely safe.

"And, as you all know," Hans added, "the Seeing Eye won't allow any dog to go to a blind person until the trainer is absolutely satisfied that the dog has learned his lessons. We put on blindfolds, and the dogs take us around town. A trainer-director follows us, rating the dog's performance. It's like taking final exams before graduation."

Hans also pointed out that if any peculiarities develop after the dog has been placed, a Seeing Eye representative pays the blind man a visit in his own home to check up on the problems. Jonathan recalled the lady and her squirrel-chasing dog guide, and wondered how many "phuis" were required to break that bad habit.

When he finished his talk, Hans spoke to his dog: "Happy, forward."

They were up and away at a fast clip, Hans waving back to the children as he disappeared into the kennels.

Jonathan felt a trifle sad, knowing that Inky would be living here one day, perhaps a part of Hans' "string." He tried to forget that the day would come when he would lose her. It was something to face later, not now. He wondered how the children around him felt — the girl who had raised five pups, for instance — when the time came to give them up. He asked her, as they munched their sandwiches.

"It hurts for a while," she told him. "Every dog is just a little bit different and special. I always hug them and kiss them when Mr. Gordon comes to get them, and tell them not to forget what I've told them. Then when he gives me another puppy, I just hug it and kiss it and tell it not to worry, and I tell it the same thing I tell all my pups."

"What's that?" asked Jonathan.

"I just tell them I love them, now and forever. Don't you?"

"No," said Jonathan, "I never thought about telling Inky."

Jonathan was inclined to think that all girls were a little silly, but he made a mental note to tell Inky that very night. Maybe she'd remember it in the years ahead.

Suddenly Mr. Gordon motioned toward The Seeing Eye school and put a finger to his lips. "Sit here quietly, folks, and watch that porch door. It will open in a minute."

They stopped talking, all eyes on the door. In a few seconds it did open. A very beautiful girl with golden curls came out. She held her head high, and she smiled confidently ahead of her. Her eyes saw nothing, but another pair of brown eyes directed her steps. They belonged to a German shepherd dog guide wearing a stiff leather harness that directed the girl. She paused at the top of the porch steps, feeling with her toe at the first riser. The dog paused until she had taken the step. Then, slowly and carefully, the dog repeated this process until all the steps had been taken. They reached the cement pavement, and the girl reached down and patted her dog. Then she said in a clear voice:

"Forward, Bonnie."

The dog walked down the path and stopped automatically at a curb. Here again the girl felt the curb with her toe, stepped down, and crossed a road leading to a large paved area.

"It's time," Mr. Gordon whispered, "for our blind students to water their dogs. Watch. There'll be more."

And as the children watched, a dozen students appeared with their dogs. Some were elderly men and women, some were men in uniforms, others were girls and boys of college age, like the first little blonde.

The dogs guided their masters and mistresses ahead and from the left with a quiet dignity, eyes ahead, alert to each problem, listening for the few words of command that would tell them the direction they were to walk.

"They know. They know," thought Jonathan, "that these people are blind."

Some of the blind people walked with assurance. They had owned dogs before and were back for new ones. Others, who had perhaps only used canes before, walked with mincing steps, not yet sure of the newfound freedom they held at the end of the harness.

Jonathan looked up at his mother. There were tears in her eyes. He touched her hand and smiled. He felt proud, knowing what Inky would mean to some blind person. Everything was all right, once again.

"Merry Christmas!"

WHEN THEY DROVE UP TO THE FARMHOUSE late that afternoon, Uncle Jim met them at the door. He handed Mrs. Jones a cable.

"It's from the Army, Jean."

For a minute, Jonathan thought his mother wasn't going to open it. She seemed to be trying to get up enough courage to read it. Finally she tore the envelope open, and her eyes flew over the message.

Then she hugged Jonathan, her eyes filled with tears.

"Oh Jonathan," she said, "everything's going to be all right. Dad's coming home."

The cable told them that Sergeant Andrew Jones

was among many United Nations soldiers who had been exchanged at the Korean front. He had been moved to a base hospital in Tokyo, Japan. As soon as possible, he would be sent home by hospital ship.

"Mom, do you think he'll be well enough to make it home for Christmas?"

His mother seemed anxious, but also relieved. "We don't know, Johnny. But he is safe and in good hands now, and that's all that matters."

Uncle Jim nodded. "Don't either of you be worrying about Andy," he said reassuringly.

Uncle Jim's words made Jonathan feel much better.

"I'm going upstairs and write Dad a letter right now," Jonathan announced. "I'll tell him all about Inky and the picnic. He's got to know about everything that's happened since he left."

Seated at his little pine desk, Jonathan took out his pencil and paper.

"Dear Dad —" he began.

Ever since his capture, no one knew for certain whether Sergeant Jones had received any letters from home. But now the words Jonathan was writing would be read by his father in a week, in Japan. How far away both Japan and his father seemed to him just then.

He couldn't imagine his father in a strange land where they ate rice and wore straw sandals and lived in paper houses. But he could see him, just as plain as he could see Inky at his side, the day he left Valley View in his uniform. He was straight and tall, and his eyes wrinkled with little webs of smile lines. Jonathan remembered his last words: "Take care of Mom till I come home."

The boy bit the end of his pencil and then wrote: "We just got the good news."

Then he wrote page after page about home and the animals, Mom and school — but mostly he wrote about Inky.

That night the little family, with Inky, walked down to the parsonage for the Harvest Dinner. Jonathan was bursting with the news about his father. As soon as he saw Father Stuart at the parsonage door, he rushed up to him.

"Dad's free. He's in a hospital in Japan. He's coming home real soon!"

"Jonathan, that's wonderful news."

Soon all the neighbors had gathered around them to hear the details. They kissed Jonathan's mother and hugged him and began to plan a homecoming celebration.

"We'll put a big red ribbon around Inky," Mrs. Jones laughed.

"And we'll have a church supper the like of which you've never seen," suggested old Mr. MacGregor.

The minister nodded. "Yes, I don't imagine Sergeant Jones ate very well in the prison camp. Jeannie, you're going to have to put some weight on him when you get him home."

The minister had once been a missionary out there and knew all about Korea. He added, "These people don't have as much to eat as you or I do, and I imagine the prisoners ate pretty much what their captors ate: rice gruel."

"And Dad hates rice," Jonathan remembered.

As winter set in, the family continued to wait for news. From week to week they received letters written by an Army nurse, taking dictation from Sergeant Jones' bedside. The letters were cheerful: Sergeant Jones' health was improving; his strength was returning; he was sitting up; he was gaining weight.

Then came the first letter written by Sergeant Jones himself. He was homesick. He couldn't get home for Christmas, but he was going on his first outing in Tokyo. He was going Christmas shopping in the bazaars.

"I'm not sure just when they'll discharge me, but I bet I beat the robins back to Valley View."

Back home, there was plenty of work on the farm. Inky was the pride of Jonathan's life. Her undercoat was thick, and her top coat was glossy as corn silk from her daily brushing and her egg-and-cod-liver-oil diet supplement. Her hindquarters were developing heavy and sure, and her muscles were hard.

She was a familiar sight in the village. The children knew her by name and patted her reverently. She had learned to watch out for cars, and began to develop a special traffic sense about crossing streets.

She was given every consideration by storekeepers in Valley View. The sign that said "No Dogs Allowed" did not apply to Inky.

"Just think," said old Mr. Booth, smoothing down his apron. "When she's guiding some blind person, she's got to help him around store counters as well as streets."

Inky became so familiar with Mr. Booth's grocery store that she knew exactly where the canned dog food was kept. She went to it immediately whenever Mrs. Jones took her marketing.

Inky also learned to ignore stray cats around town, and to snub the cur dogs who lived down by the railroad station. When they came yipping up to her for a fight, she curled her lips, gave a deep growl, and walked slowly by them. Mr. Gordon told Jonathan that when The Seeing Eye dogs were taking their training at Morristown, they had to go

94

through Dog Town, one of the hardest challenges. Here, as in Valley View, stray dogs tried to pick fights with the dog guides. These Seeing Eye dogs were taught — as Inky instinctively seemed to know — to ignore their tormenters with a calm show of strength.

Even the trainmen at the station sometimes let Jonathan and Inky walk through cars on the siding. Perhaps, if Inky's master were a commuter, Inky would have to know how to manage the narrow, awkward train steps.

With Jonathan, she soon learned to mount the steps, thread her way through the car, and dismount at the rear. Even a sudden whistle from a locomotive failed to startle her. She was a wonderful dog, Jonathan discovered, and the years of breeding behind her were beginning to show.

Christmas excitement really began, as far as Jonathan was concerned, the day the big brown paper package arrived from Japan. After that, Christmas began to spread. In the village, the fire department festooned gay lights along Main and South streets. Christmas carols welled out across the town from loudspeakers in the stores. The church choir practiced the special numbers they would serenade townspeople with on Christmas Eve. The first snow spread a white cover upon the trees and upper slopes of the Jones farm. Winter hayrides began along back roads, and ice skating on the ponds.

Inside the cozy farmhouse, a cricket moved into the hearth, and Inky spent hours with her nose to the crack in the fireplace from which the little insect sang his merry song.

One day Jonathan was surprised to see Mr. Mac-Gregor stomping along the path followed by his now agile, shaggy shadow, Glamis. The farmer held out a beautifully turned dog collar with Inky's name in large brass studs.

"I made it for your friend," he said gruffly. "It's a shame, the ratty thing you make that fine animal wear."

Once, during a Christmas party at Sunday school, when Inky had quietly settled herself by a warm stove, the minister patted her head.

"Children," he said, "do you know where the expression 'the seeing eye' comes from?"

Then he explained — because no one did know — that it was a quotation from the Bible, from the Book of Proverbs: "The hearing ear and the seeing eye, the Lord hath made even both of them."

"What I think the Bible means by this," he explained, "is that God has given all you children ears and eyes, and through these you hear and see all the wonderful things God created for you. You must use these gifts. He gave you your eyes and ears to understand all about God and the world He has created, how great He is, how dependent we are upon Him."

The minister pointed out that some people in the world were less fortunate, because they were either blind or deaf, or both.

"For our deaf people, we have hearing aids and other methods of communication. For our blind — well, we have dogs like Inky here. Inky will someday be the seeing eye for someone who will be in desperate need of her."

Christmas Day itself finally came to Valley View. At church, Jonathan and his mother, with Inky at their side, knelt and prayed for the quick return of Sergeant Jones.

At home under the lighted tree, they opened their presents. The packages from Japan were wrapped in strange red and gold paper, not a bit like Christmas paper in America, but still Christmas in an oriental way.

For Mrs. Jones there was a beautiful little tea set and a silk kimono. Jonathan opened his package to find a shiny camera, a Japanese edition of a German Leica. On the card, his father wrote that in the camera was a roll of exposed film he'd taken on his last visit to a little town called Nara, where tame deer came and ate from his hand.

There was also a present for Inky. It was a supple leather leash, braided intricately in several colors. It was coiled around a phonograph record to protect the record itself from breaking.

In no time Jonathan had found the old family phonograph in the attic, and he set it up under the tree. He placed the record on it, wound it up, and then the three sat by excitedly as the record began.

"Hello Jeannie and Jonathan and Inky. I miss you all very much." His father's voice sounded tired but happy. "Inky, I know all about you. I know you and Jonathan are taking care of Mom and the farm, and I'll be home soon to help you do it.

"There are a lot of beautiful German shepherds here in Japan, but I have told people that you are head and tail above them all. This leash was braided by a blind man, Inky. He lost his sight in the last world war. He is a good Japanese friend of mine, and he says he would like to come to Morristown someday and get a Seeing Eye dog like you. He can hardly believe what I tell him about you. He sends this leash with the hope you will lead a happy life.

"Merry Christmas to you all. *Sayonara* — that's 'good-bye for now' in Japanese."

Home at Last

THE LITTLE VILLAGE OF VALLEY VIEW was decked out with Fourth of July flags and bunting on that cold February morning when Sergeant Jones' train arrived from Newark.

The firemen's band, muffled in heavy overcoats, huddled in the waiting room of the station. The mayor and his wife, Mrs. Jones with Jonathan and Inky, walked up and down the platform with a crowd of friends. Their breath was frosty, noses were red, and occasionally Mrs. Jones dabbed her eyes as the time narrowed down to five minutes before train time.

Excitement had been mounting at the Jones farm

ever since the cable came on New Year's Day telling them that Sergeant Jones was on his way home aboard a hospital ship. It was still hard to believe that in a few minutes he would actually step off the train and be in Valley View.

Suddenly Jonathan saw Inky prick up her ears. "Mom, she hears the train," he shouted. "She can hear eight times better than we can."

And sure enough, seconds later they all heard the train sounding a warning toot around the bend. It soon chugged noisily into sight and squealed to a slow halt at the station platform. The band by now had trooped out and begun to tune up their instruments. A trainman alighted and placed a small stand on the platform. Then he went back to the coach and helped a man in a khaki greatcoat to alight.

His family and friends watched proudly as Sergeant Jones turned to face them. The band started up "America," and the high school principal ran up the school flag. At the sight of the colors, the sergeant came to a brief, stiff salute. Then he saw his wife and son running toward him, and he held out his arms. "Jeannie, Johnny, at last."

Sergeant Jones held his wife tenderly. Then he turned and looked down at Jonathan and Inky. The

boy saw that his father was thin and pale, a trifle un-
steady on his feet. But his eyes were warm and
smiling.

"Jeannie, I can't believe it. I'm home."

It seemed all he could say. He came close to them
to study their faces with eager, homesick eyes. Inky,
nudging him gently, almost upset his balance. He
patted her.

"Why, hello there, Inky," he said. And then to
his proud son, he added, "She is a beauty, Jonathan."

Then the band started to play a march, and they all got into the mayor's car and drove through the street while friends came out and waved and cheered and called to the sergeant.

They had a reception at the schoolhouse and the biggest lunch ever served at the church guild. There was so much food that Sergeant Jones could only nibble at the turkey and roast beef and potato salad, the bread and jelly, the homemade pies and cakes sent over by practically every housekeeper in Valley View.

Sergeant Jones just sat at the head table and stared at his plate. "We have so much to be thankful for," he told his friends. "I only wish we could share all this with the less fortunate men who are still in prison camps."

There was little the family could say until they finally reached home and the last of the visitors had said good-bye.

Then the sergeant sank into his favorite chair by the fire.

"You'll have to forgive me, Jeannie, but I used up my last ounce of strength at the guild hall. I'm terribly, terribly tired."

Mrs. Jones tucked a robe around his legs. "I know, Andy, and you are going to get nothing but rest and quiet and good food. You'll be up and around in no time."

Sergeant Jones seemed to drift off for a few minutes, then he shook himself. "I just can't believe I'm home," he said. "It's been such a nightmare. Where are you, Jeannie?"

He looked around as if expecting to waken from a dream. His wife came and put her arms around him and kissed him.

"I'll be all right in a month or so. Doctor said to take it easy. Then we'll get things started around the farm." With this, he drifted off to sleep.

The days lengthened into weeks as Andrew Jones fought back to health with rest and good food and the skilled medical treatment the nearby Veterans Hospital afforded. Eventually he began to put on weight. His stooping shoulders straightened and he didn't waken as often during the night, trembling and perspiring.

Spring came earlier that year, and by March the sergeant was able to sit out and sun himself on the protected porch near Inky's kennel. Jonathan watched and waited for the time when his father would be able to do things again with him. He wanted to plan a great season of muskrat trapping down in the marshy bottom land. He wanted to plan a camp-out with Charlie and his dad. He wanted to work out a 4-H project to raise pheasants for the state. There was so much to talk about, but his father would always wave him away gently and tell him to wait.

Gradually both Jonathan and his mother realized that there was something still missing from the man who had once been so vigorous and keen. It was more than just poor physical condition. Something new seemed to bother Andrew Jones, something he was keeping to himself. Then one day Jonathan learned what it was.

Mrs. Jones had gone off marketing that bright

spring morning, and Jonathan was in the barn cleaning the stalls. He saw his father walking toward him in the shadows.

"I seem to feel more at home in dark places, Jonathan," he said, sitting down on a bale of hay. "I guess I'm not used to sunlight yet. They kept me cooped up in that dark cell for so long."

He was holding out a letter which had been opened. "Johnny, the mail just came. Read this for me like a good boy."

Jonathan looked at his father strangely. "Sure Dad, but —"

Sergeant Jones was abrupt. "Just read it, son. The light outside was too bright."

The letter was from the Army doctor in the department of ophthalmology. Jonathan couldn't pronounce it, but he spelled it out slowly.

His father was impatient. "Yes, yes, that's the eye doc, Jonathan. What does he say?"

Johnny continued. The doctor's letter explained that the recent tests at the hospital revealed that Sergeant Andrew Jones had developed an optic atrophy. That meant a degeneration of the optic nerve resulting from starvation while in prison. The optic nerve was the special nerve of sight, connecting the eye and the optic centers of the brain.

"Because of malnutrition," the doctor wrote, "the

optic nerve has finally atrophied, or disintegrated. The loss of central vision is the result. I am sorry to say, this will mean almost total blindness."

Jonathan's father had slumped down in the hay, head buried in hands. He didn't notice Jonathan's arm on his shoulder. He didn't speak.

Jonathan remained with his father until the jeep braked in the driveway and he heard his mother calling. He went out to her with the letter. She read it quickly, and her breath caught. "Oh, Johnny, your poor father." Then she ran to the barn.

Jonathan and Inky watched her go into the barn. Then she came out with Jonathan's father, and they both went into the house. Jonathan sat down by Inky, buried his face in her rough fur, and cried. He knew now what a terrible fear had been tormenting his father. Inky put her head on his shoulder, as if trying to be as close to him as possible. Gradually Jonathan's tears stopped. Then he looked at Inky with a new hope.

"Perhaps, perhaps, oh Inky —"

He jumped to his feet and raced toward the house. He knew now what he could do to help his father. Up in his room at his desk, he struggled to write the letter to Mr. Gordon that would mean his father's salvation.

"I know," he began, "that Inky's a very valuable

dog. You probably want her for somebody special, who can give her a wonderful home. But if it's possible, could you ask The Seeing Eye if my father might have Inky? He's almost blind. I don't know what Inky will cost, but I know I can earn the money."

Then realizing how much he was asking, Jonathan wrote a timid P.S.: "If not Inky, perhaps there might be another dog for him who isn't quite as perfect."

Jonathan mailed the letter Monday on his way to school. He wanted to have the privilege of telling his father, in the event Mr. Gordon granted his request and he was able to get Inky. He also wanted to shield him from any disappointment if the request was turned down. He remembered that Mr. Gordon once told him that the school did not allow 4-H members or anyone else to raise a Seeing Eye dog for a family member. Each dog had to be matched to his master, and only wise trainers knew how to do this.

However, Jonathan risked telling his secret hopes to Inky, who after all, knew all his other secrets.

Unhappy Days

THE WEEK THAT FOLLOWED was the unhappiest Jonathan had ever known.

His father retreated to his bedroom and stayed there alone. Mrs. Jones took all his meals up to him and sat with him as long as she could between household chores. Jonathan continued to work about the farm before and after school. But the bedroom door was closed to him and to Inky.

One afternoon on his way home from school, Jonathan met the minister just leaving the farmhouse. "Your father's a sick man," Father Stuart said sadly. "It's the hardest sickness there is to cure, for it is in his heart and mind."

The next day the doctor from the Veterans Hospital came and examined Jonathan's father. He confirmed everything the family feared. His father was almost totally blind. It would be only a matter of weeks.

"I'm afraid, Mrs. Jones," he added, "that you are going to have to make him want to live again, as a blind man. This final blow has been almost too much after everything else he's been through."

The next few days passed slowly, and still no word came from Mr. Gordon and The Seeing Eye. Jonathan hardly ever saw his mother. She made his breakfast, laid out his clothes for school, wrote lists of groceries for him to buy in town. Most of her days she spent with her husband, behind the closed door.

Finally, on Saturday night, still without word from The Seeing Eye, Jonathan decided that he must talk to his father. He made this decision when he came back from a final check at the mailbox to find his mother with tears in her eyes. Maybe it would help everyone, he decided, if he talked to his father about that letter he'd written.

He walked slowly up the steps to the bedroom. Inky followed, her toenails clickety-clacking on the bare floors. The door was slightly ajar. Jonathan pushed it open. His father was sitting up in a chair, fully dressed, staring sightlessly out the window. There was no light in the room except the fire shadows from the open hearth. Outside, a storm was brewing, and Jonathan heard the trees whipping in the wind. A white storm light spread over the farm, and below he saw swirls of leaves dancing in the yard. He was glad the animals were safely bedded down. It could be a bad storm, the radio said, with high winds and heavy rain.

"Hello, Dad." Jonathan felt awkward for the first time in his father's presence. "Inky and I came up to talk to you."

His father did not seem to hear him.

Jonathan put his arm on his father's shoulder. Then, after a long pause, Jonathan began to tell his father about the letter. Perhaps, just knowing it had been written and mailed might bring him new hope.

"Dad, just think, maybe you can have a dog guide, even if it isn't Inky."

Jonathan was dumfounded by his father's reaction. The sergeant lashed out at his son. "I'd shoot myself before I would be as helpless as that."

Before Jonathan could protest, his father pushed him away. The boy lost his balance and fell down.

Inky, quick as a streak of lightning, leaped up to protect the boy. She turned on his father, growling, hackles up. In the noise and confusion, Sergeant Jones kicked out blindly toward Inky with his heavy Army boot. She yipped with quick pain. Jonathan reached out for her, sobbing.

"You'd better go, both of you," his father commanded.

Jonathan and Inky went toward the door, carefully avoiding the crouched figure in the chair. The boy bumped headlong into his mother, who was standing just outside, her face white and frightened. "She must have seen it all," thought Jonathan, "but she has nothing to say to me." He pushed past her and fled to his own room, Inky at his side.

Behind locked door, Jonathan carefully examined his beloved pet. There was a slight cut above Inky's eye, but she was otherwise unharmed. If the blow had not been a glancing one, it might have inflicted severe damage.

Outside, the storm was mounting, and hard-driven raindrops splattered against the windows. Miserable and unhappy, Jonathan made a decision. He had to run away. He would get as far as he could before the full fury of the storm hit. Perhaps, with luck, he could make Mr. MacGregor's barn and

sleep there in the hayloft until dawn. After that, he and Inky would go on; he didn't care where.

Jonathan pulled boots over his dungarees, put on an extra sweater and his flight jacket. Into a Scout knapsack he stuffed Inky's biscuits for the next day's trip and some candy bars for himself. He heard angry voices behind the bedroom door as he stepped into the hall and made his way quietly downstairs. He took one extra can of dog food from the kitchen, and then with Inky he pushed outside into the stormy night. Inky was free, but she kept close to Jonathan.

It was a long, cold, stumbling walk up the hills toward the MacGregor farm. By now the storm was hitting all around the valley. There was jagged lightning followed by bursts of thunder. Then came the downpour of rain. It was long after midnight when they finally reached the farmer's stone fence boundary, clambered over the cold, wet rocks, and made for the barn. It loomed up, dark but inviting, against the white light of the spring gale.

Once inside the barn, the warmth of the sheep revived Jonathan's numbed body. He heard Glamis bark shrilly from the farmhouse and saw the lights go on for a few minutes in the farmer's bedroom.

He helped his wet dog up into the lower loft and

followed her, snuggling down in the soft, fragrant hay. He covered up carefully so nothing showed above the hay but Inky's nose and his own face. Then, exhausted, he fell into a sound sleep.

Sometime during the stormy night, Jonathan thought he heard Inky growl softly. But he did not awaken when a pencil of light from Farmer Mac-Gregor's flashlight played on his face, or when two cold noses of sheepdog and German shepherd met in quiet recognition. The farmer snapped off his light, smiled sadly to himself, and then went back to his house.

Early the next morning, Mr. MacGregor made a phone call to his good friend, Mr. Gordon, because the phone connection to the Jones farm was out. Then, whistling to Glamis, he went out to the barn and woke up the runaway boy.

"I've some porridge for you, lad," he grinned, as Jonathan opened his eyes. "If it's running away you're up to, you had better not do it on an empty stomach."

An Important Decision

AFTER TWO BOWLS OF OATMEAL and at least four slices of bread and strawberry jam, Jonathan began to wonder whether it might not be just as pleasant to live with Mr. MacGregor and become a shepherd. He raised the question carefully, with as little explanation as possible.

"You see, sir, my father doesn't want me any more. Would you give me a job tending your sheep? Of course, Inky could work too."

The farmer took a deep draw on his pipe and stared out the window, meditating. The storm had long ago spent itself, and the bright sunshine of early spring filtered through the window. It was warm and promising.

"We might arrange it, son," the old man finally said. "But I thought Inky belonged to The Seeing Eye people."

Jonathan's responsibility to Mr. Gordon suddenly returned, sharply in focus. Inky was almost ready to start her training. One day soon, Jonathan would have to give her up and she would begin the work she was born to do. He shook his head sadly. "I forgot, just for a minute."

The farmer nodded. "I know how it is, lad. But I think it would be only proper if you notify The Seeing Eye people just where you might be reached when that day arrives for them to come and get your fine beasty."

The boy agreed. "I suppose I could write Mr. Gordon."

"Better yet, Jonathan, why don't you go back to your father's farm and leave word where you are. I'm sure they'll all be grateful if you do that. Then you can come back here and start work Monday."

Jonathan agreed reluctantly. He didn't like the idea of going home so soon after last night's scene. But again, there was that nagging sense of duty. Of course he'd have to let Mr. Gordon know where to find Inky. And he would need some more clothes.

The trip home that morning was much easier

than his flight in the night. Robins were cocking their heads for fresh worms loamed up by the rain. Yellow violets peered out from glossy clusters of heart-shaped leaves. The sun was getting warmer.

Inky romped ahead, sniffing the new earth and the growing things. She paused tentatively before some skunk cabbages, those first signs of spring, but Jonathan urged her on. He remembered her first meeting with a real skunk, and wondered vaguely why such a lady as Inky should like such odd perfume.

Far, far away he heard the church bells in the village. His mother was probably in church now, sitting alone for the first time. Jonathan felt a little bad about that, and he didn't want to face her. Perhaps, if he hurried, he could get there before she returned from church. He would leave a note, explaining everything. It would be easier that way.

At the edge of the farm, Jonathan heard the unhappy cackling of cooped-up chickens. No one had fed them. Running for the coop, he was greeted by affectionate cluckings on all side. The scuppers were empty, the water pans dry. He soon tended their simple needs and freed them to the chicken yard. From habit, he scooped up twelve eggs and left the coop.

On the way, Jonathan watered and fed the rest of the stock. They had been waiting patiently for someone to come, and they all seemed perplexed at what was going on in the human kingdom. Jonathan realized how upset his mother must have been when she discovered he had left home. She never neglected the animals.

The boy was surprised to see the familiar green truck in the driveway. Sitting on the front steps was Mr. Gordon talking to Mrs. Jones. At the sight of her son, Mrs. Jones ran toward him, swept him into her arms, and kissed him.

"Oh, Johnny, Johnny, we are both so sorry. Your father and I have been worried all night. I'll go right up and tell him you're back home."

She left them, calling upstairs to her husband. Jonathan looked sheepishly at Mr. Gordon, who grinned back at him and Inky.

"Hi there, you two. How are you?"

He patted Inky and then turned seriously to Jonathan. "I only got your letter yesterday. I was downstate on business all week."

The boy squirmed uncomfortably. "I guess it doesn't matter now, one way or another. Dad doesn't — doesn't want any help."

Mr. Gordon nodded sympathetically. "I know,

Johnny, I've been talking to your mother. But there are a few things we have to discuss, you and I, about The Seeing Eye and how it operates."

Johnny sat down next to his friend on the stoop. "It's really okay, Mr. Gordon. I never should have asked for Inky in the first place."

Mr. Gordon interrupted: "Jonathan, you see, in the first place, it is impossible for me to promise Inky to anyone. She goes to the man or woman who is best suited for her temperament, and vice versa. It won't be any special person with a lot of money or a beautiful home."

Then he explained that when a blind person applied to The Seeing Eye for a dog, he was given individual study. Sometimes the blind didn't qualify to have a dog because of some physical disability. Some just didn't like dogs. But when a blind person was finally passed by The Seeing Eye board, he and his dog were carefully matched. If he had a gentle disposition, his dog was gentle. If he was gruff, his dog was a little firmer in make-up.

Mr. Gordon continued: "Each blind student who comes to the Seeing Eye shares in the cost of his dogs: 150 dollars for the first dog, 50 dollars for succeeding ones. Payments may be deferred," he said, "and no one has ever been denied a dog for

current lack of funds. Seeing Eye graduates refer to their sharing in expenses as 'payments on self-respect.' We make an exception for veterans — men who have lost their sight in the service of their country — they are given dogs free. It's a sort of debt of gratitude we all feel toward such men."

Engrossed in their talk, neither Jonathan nor Mr. Gordon heard the footsteps behind them. Sergeant Jones and his wife stopped at the front screen door and listened.

"But you don't understand, Mr. Gordon. Dad doesn't want a dog." The boy's voice was full of tears. "It's like what the minister said. He won't fight back any more. Is that being a coward?"

"Jonathan, we can't label it cowardice. Your father was a brave man. This last blow was just too much for him."

There was a pause, as if Mr. Gordon was trying to be kind. Then he continued: "Jonathan, I'm very sorry, but I am afraid The Seeing Eye would not give your father a dog. Not if he were the richest man in the world, or the most important. You see, *we only give Seeing Eye dogs to people who want to help themselves.*"

Suddenly the porch door snapped open. Sergeant Jones felt his way out into the warm sunlight. Both Jonathan and Mr. Gordon jumped up.

The blind man held out his arms. "Where are you both? Let me sit beside you."

Mr. Gordon took the sergeant's arm and led him expertly down the steps. Jonathan sat beside him, half frightened. His father sensed his feelings.

"Johnny, first of all, I want you to know how sorry I am about last night. When we found you'd run away, I was shocked back to my senses."

He put a tender arm around Jonathan, and the boy stared, embarrassed, down at his feet.

The sergeant turned to Mr. Gordon. "I heard everything you two said, and most of it is absolutely true. I don't deserve help, but I'm going to ask for it anyway."

There was a long, unhappy pause. The sergeant stared straight ahead into the darkness of the space around him. Finally he turned again to The Seeing Eye man.

"I would like to ask you to reconsider, Mr. Gordon. I want to prove to Jonathan that his father can fight back. Let your board at The Seeing Eye decide if I am qualified for a dog guide. Just give me one chance."

Mr. Gordon looked from Jonathan to the sergeant's anxious, war-weary face. Finally he said, "All I can do is to place your request before our board. They will decide."

123

"Fair enough," said the sergeant, and reached out his hand. The two men shook hands, and Mr. Gordon quietly placed the soldier's hand on Inky's coat. "Get used to the feel of a dog at your feet, Sergeant. Maybe one day a dog like Inky will be there, waiting to help you, if you really want to help yourself."

Sergeant Jones reached down and ran his fingers through Inky's thick fur. She seemed to understand the questioning touch of a blind man. She arose and placed herself on her haunches next to him at his feet.

"I'm sorry, Inky girl, about last night." The sergeant whispered to her.

Then before anyone realized what Mr. Gordon was saying, he had stood up and addressed Jonathan: "Johnny, I have bad news for you. This is the day I have to take Inky away from you. You remember, I warned you one day this would happen."

As he spoke, he slipped Inky's leather collar off and placed a chain choke collar around her. Inky looked questioningly at Jonathan. The boy put his arms around her, fighting back tears. He held her for a minute, and then looked up at Mr. Gordon.

"Please sir, don't put her in the cage behind. Can she ride with you?"

124

"Of course, Johnny. Inky's going to ride where she belongs. Right up front."

Before they realized it, the green truck, Mr. Gordon, and Inky had gone. The three who were left sat quietly in the spring sunshine, drawn together even more closely now because of the loss they felt. Nothing could ever replace the merry brown eyes, the happy bark, the companionship of a great and loving dog like Inky.

A Wonderful Surprise

THE DAYS THAT FOLLOWED INKY'S DEPARTURE were lonely ones for Jonathan, but busy ones too. His father was becoming more and more the man he remembered before Korea. He joined Jonathan at every opportunity, and they planned the spring planting, a trapping expedition to the marshes, new projects for the summer ahead. More important, the sergeant began to learn to read Braille. His first success was telling time by the nubs on a watch for the blind. More and more lessons and records arrived from the Veterans Hospital, and as the weeks went by, the sergeant announced that he was nearly through first grade in Braille and would soon be catching up to Jonathan.

It was early May when they received the letter from The Seeing Eye people. Sergeant Jones had been accepted as a member of the class forming in early June. Schoolwork would be intensive if he passed his tests, and The Seeing Eye people hoped that the sergeant would arrive in top physical condition. Long walks, they suggested, would help to develop leg muscles and tone up the entire body.

As the time approached for his father to leave, Jonathan tried not to think how lonely it would be without him. It was hard enough trying to forget Inky. And now he had to lose his newfound father.

"Don't worry, Jonathan," his mother told them both. "We know Dad will pass the tests, and think how much more he can do when he has a guide dog to take him places. He can take those extension courses at the university, develop a new herd of cows, really make the old farm pay. His eyes just need a cold nose."

It was agreed that Sergeant Jones would go to The Seeing Eye school with a representative who would drive up from the school. Then, on graduation day, the family would drive down and pick him up. In this way the busy farm life would not be interrupted, and the sergeant could start out at once to devote his entire energies to learning a new way of life.

On the appointed day, a pleasant young man and a trainer arrived in a station wagon. The trainer explained that he would start work immediately with his new student, getting acquainted on the trip down to school.

As they loaded the sergeant's baggage into the car, Jonathan screwed up his courage and asked the trainer in a voice he meant to sound disinterested, "Do you know a dog named Inky, down there in training?"

The trainer looked carefully at Jonathan and smiled. "You raise Inky, Johnny?"

The boy's voice quavered. "Yes sir, and Mr. Gordon says she's a wonderfully smart dog."

The man shook his head. "I'm afraid Inky isn't on my string. Most likely, if she's that smart, she must be placed by now. We have a lot of dogs — a lot of good dogs. But I'm sorry I didn't meet Inky."

Jonathan didn't like that. Inky, his special Inky, just one of many good dogs. Maybe she was working now with some blind master. He hoped she was happy.

Meanwhile The Seeing Eye official explained to the family that students kept close to their work for the first week and saw no one. During this period they would be studied by the school personnel and graded according to their ability to work with dogs.

"We'll let you know if the sergeant needs anything — like extra shoes or toothpaste," the official promised. "And don't worry about him. He'll be in good hands and feet."

During the four long weeks that followed, Jonathan's mother received weekly notes from the school. The first said that Sergeant Jones had passed all requirements and would be assigned a dog suitable to his temperament. Shortly afterward Sergeant Jones wrote a hasty note. They were trying him out on a boxer named Peggy, who seemed very gentle and smart. He was busy every minute of his waking day, and would try and write again if he could beg or borrow the time. His writing wasn't up to scratch, but he was learning to type. His roommate was also teaching him to play the piano, which Peggy seemed to relish. "She sings, off key, with us," he wrote. That was the last word they heard from him until graduation. Then they received a nicely typed note inviting them to pick up "one sergeant and dog, about to be discharged from the Seeing Eye school."

Graduation Day was a bright and wonderful Fourth of July, and Jonathan remembered on the long drive to the school another beautiful day when they had first visited The Seeing Eye. Jonathan wondered if Mr. Gordon would ever tell him what had happened to Inky. Perhaps it was better not to know. He told himself sternly that he had said good-bye to Inky when he closed her 4-H record book and mailed it to Mr. Gordon.

Jonathan was heartsick, nevertheless, when they turned into the school driveway and he saw the beautiful German shepherds at play in their runs. They brought back so many memories of Inky — the way they danced and barked and loped and held their heads.

Driving up to the school building, Jonathan pointed out a familiar green truck. "Look, Mom, there's Mr. Gordon on the steps."

The Seeing Eye man greeted them warmly and motioned them into the school. "The students are getting spruced up a bit for their last day here," he told them. "They don't just learn how to work with dog guides. They learn to put on their clothes properly, tie their ties, straighten the seams in their stockings, and put on lipstick. Wait and see."

Mr. Gordon introduced Mrs. Jones and Jonathan to some of the other families who were waiting for the graduates. He showed them all around the lounge and adjoining rooms. In one corner he pointed out the physical layout of the school, worked in bas relief so that the blind could study their campus with their finger tips.

The life-size picture of Buddy Fortunate Fields, the first Seeing Eye dog, hung in the hallway and reminded Jonathan again of his Inky. "Buddy was a most important immigrant." Mr. Gordon pointed to the picture. "She came from Switzerland to prove to America that guide dogs could function in this mechanized country."

Jonathan found himself confiding to a very handsome lady that Buddy looked just like his Inky. The lady smiled and said she didn't know much about shepherds because her husband, who was getting his second dog, had used only Labradors. "They like our Chicago climate," she said.

An elderly Negro lady joined them. "My boy doesn't care what kind he gets, as long as the dog doesn't mind music. He's a piano player, and the whole band is excited about his dog. He'll travel all over with them."

Mr. Gordon assured her that her son had probably received a very musical dog who would more than likely harmonize from time to time with the band.

"We had a letter from a blind lecturer the other day. He says his dog joins in the applause at the end by standing up and barking."

Mr. Gordon also told them something about how the students lived. They shared dormitories on the floor above, and each one kept his dog at his bed-side at night, chained. During mealtime they all sat in the communal dining room, where the eating utensils were set at prearranged locations, so there would be a minimum of confusion. After school hours the students played cards or musical instruments or listened to the radio, if they weren't too tired from their day's activities.

"But they should be coming down any second now," he added. "Let's go out in the foyer, where we can see them walk down the steps with their dogs."

The little group was mustered out to the foyer and stood watching silently as the first blind student made his appearance at the head of the stairs. He was a nicely dressed young man with a magnificent black Labrador retriever. That, thought Jonathan, would be the man from Chicago. He walked confidently to the landing, and his wife went to him, arms outstretched. She embraced both the man and his new dog.

The Negro piano player followed, with a golden boxer in harness.

And then, in his starched khaki uniform, came Sergeant Andrew Jones.

Jonathan's mother ran to her husband, tears in

her eyes. But Jonathan saw only the great black and tan dog walking so confidently at his side. *It was Inky!*

All her weeks of rigid training were forgotten when Inky saw Jonathan. The sergeant braced himself and began to run with the dog, as if expecting just such a reaction.

"Nobody has to tell me where Jonathan is," he said, reaching out for his son. "See what a surprise I've been saving for you?"

"Oh Dad, you got her, you got Inky!" Jonathan was still unbelieving. "Isn't it wonderful?"

Tears trickled down his face as he watched Inky regain her composure and stand obediently at his father's side in a shiny leather harness.

"I worked very hard for her, Jonathan," his father said. "Peggy just wasn't my type. She's really a musician at heart, and fell in love with the piano player. Then the trainer brought me Inky. He tells me we made a perfect team right from the start."

Behind them, Jonathan heard Mr. Gordon's familiar voice. "Jonathan, here's something I've been meaning to give you."

He held out a silver medal with the outline of the German shepherd engraved on it. The inscription said that Jonathan had raised a puppy for The Seeing Eye.

Mr. Gordon walked out with them to the jeep, watching Sergeant Jones with Inky. The sergeant walked like a soldier, with his head up, shoulders out, his springy step in rhythm with Inky's own walk. He was confident and happy, and it reflected in his face.

Mr. Gordon was grinning broadly as they neared the jeep. "Johnny," he said, "Can you stand one more shock?"

But the boy saw it first, sitting on the front seat of the jeep, smiling, wiggling, yipping. It was a four-month-old edition of Inky! Mr. Gordon went over and patted the pup.

"She's Inky's sister, Jonathan. We didn't know whether you wanted to raise another one or not . . ."

Before he could finish the sentence, Jonathan had leaped into the jeep and his arms were around the new puppy.

Inky looked on with interest, wagging her tail. Jonathan's mother and father were both laughing.

"You name her, Johnny," Mr. Gordon said. "Anything starting with L."

"Lindy," suggested Mrs. Jones.

"Liza," said her husband.

But Jonathan didn't care what she was called. To him, she was Inky as a puppy, come back to love all over again.

Note to the Reader

A New Home for The Seeing Eye

When this story was written, The Seeing Eye was housed in an old Victorian building on Whippany Road, in Morristown, New Jersey. Several years later The Seeing Eye moved to new quarters on the other side of town. Now the school is in a beautiful two-story building on a hill overlooking historic Washington Valley. Here the students live in comfortable modern rooms, instead of dormitories, and have many lounges for relaxing and parks for walking their dogs.

The program of The Seeing Eye is much the same today as it was when the school was in its old quarters. And the 4-H club members of New Jersey are still one of the most important parts of the program. Boys and girls — like Jonathan in this book — help raise The Seeing Eye puppies until they are ready to be trained to serve their new masters.